TIMELESS LOVE

"It would not matter to me who you were. I realised that whatever the consequences, I could not live without you."

He then kissed her fiercely, demandingly, as if he was still afraid he might lose her and the agonies he had suffered when he tried to do so were still making him afraid.

"I love you!" he said when he raised his head. "I love you so much that I cannot think of anything except that you will be my wife and we will be together as fate intended us to be since the moment I saw you."

Bantam Books by Barbara Cartland
Ask your bookseller for the books you have missed

Barbara Cartland's Library of Love Series

The Waltz
Of
Hearts

Barbara Cartland

BANTAM BOOKS
TORONTO · NEW YORK · LONDON

THE WALTZ OF HEARTS
A Bantam Book / May 1981

ISBN 0–553–14586–X

Published simultaneously in the United States and Canada

Bantam Books are published by Bantam Books, Inc. Its trade-
mark, consisting of the words "Bantam Books" and the por-
trayal of a bantam, is Registered in U.S. Patent and Trademark
Office and in other countries. Marca Registrada. Bantam
Books, Inc., 666 Fifth Avenue, New York, New York 10103.

PRINTED IN THE UNITED STATES OF AMERICA

0 9 8 7 6 5 4 3 2 1

Author's Note

When I visited Vienna the first time, I loved the *Heurigers* Wine-gardens, where the music was as I have described in this novel, the inspiring St. Stephen's Cathedral, and the charming good manners of the Austrians.

Later I wrote *The Private Life of Elizabeth, Empress of Austria,* which for many years was acknowledged by the Elizabeth Club to be the best biography of her.

A further honour came in 1969 when I was given a Civic Reception for my work for the Health Movement by the Mayor of Vienna who, during the war, had served in the Resistance with President Tito and Dr. Paul Urban.

There was a delicious and impressive dinner in the historic *Rathaus* (City Hall), and when the speeches were over, a band appeared and we all danced "The Blue Danube."

The Esterházy Palace still stands in the small village of Fertöd. It was badly damaged in the last war. The summer-houses and ornamental temples in the French Rococo Park, once part of the background of the *Udvar*—the old Court world—were largely destroyed. But restoration on the magnificent Palace itself is now complete. It is one of the great sights of Hungary and attracts over 100,000 tourists each year.

Chapter One

1873

"I am tired, Gisela."

"Then you must go to bed, Papa."

"That is what I intend to do."

"I am sure you will sleep well here in the woods."

The large, fat Proprietress of the Inn, coming into the room at that moment with a pot of steaming-hot coffee in her hand, heard what Gisela had said.

"You will not be awakened, *Herr* Ferraris. I have given you a room at the back, and it is impossible to hear from there what is going on in the front, however noisy my young guests might be."

"You have always been kindness itself, *Frau* Bubna," Paul Ferraris replied.

The Proprietress, putting the coffee down on the table, smiled at him affectionately.

"I shall never forget when I first saw you, a thin snippet of a lad you were, a new student at the University and rather afraid of what would happen to you. But when I heard you play—!"

She threw up her hands.

"Then I knew unmistakably that you were a genius!"

"You were the only one who recognised it in those days!"

"I am never mistaken," *Frau* Bubna said, shaking

1

her finger at him. "Never—never! And with you there was no chance of my making a mistake."

Gisela clasped her hands together.

She knew it made her father happy to hear such things said to him in his beloved Austria, where he had studied at the University of Vienna.

On the way he had talked of nothing but the people who had been kind to him as a young man and how he hoped they were still alive.

They had arrived in Vienna early that afternoon, after a long, tiring train journey that seemed as if it would never end.

They had taken a carriage out of the city and up into the Vienna Woods to the Inn where Paul Ferraris had said he would be welcome even after twenty-five years.

Gisela had been half-afraid that the place would be closed or would have changed hands, and she knew how much that would disappoint her father.

However, after only a moment's hesitation at the sight of him, when he said his name *Frau* Bubna had flung her arms round him and exclaimed:

"It's my scraggy little Paul, the Englishman who was afraid of Vienna but who could play the violin like an angel. Welcome back! Welcome!"

After that there had been reminiscences, toasts, and news of people who were only names to Gisela.

She was very content to listen and know that her father seemed to be in better health and happier than she had seen him since her mother had died.

For over two years they had wandered from place to place, settling nowhere, and only when it seemed that their money was going to run out because he had earned so little did her father say:

"We will go to Vienna. It is where I have always meant to return, but your mother preferred France."

It was Gisela's mother who had looked after everything these past years. Her husband might make

2

the music of angels, but he had no idea that those who relied on him had to eat.

He would play for his wife and his daughter, an audience of two, as contentedly and brilliantly as if he were playing in a packed Theatre.

Paul Ferraris had been acclaimed in Paris, and with his wife organising his engagements he had made a lot of money until the outbreak of the Franco-Prussian War, and when the Germans had marched in, those who could afford it had left as quickly as they possibly could.

Quite soon afterwards his wife died very tragically after a sudden illness, and Paul Ferraris and Gisela spent a short time in the South of France.

But there was very little money to be made there, and after they moved through Italy to Greece, finally Paul Ferraris had yearned for Austria and especially for Vienna.

Gisela, trying to take her mother's place, asked him whom they should approach to arrange a Concert for him or an engagement in one of the best Theatres.

"They will know my name, there is no doubt about that," he said. "All we have to do is to contact my friends."

When Gisela pressed him for their names, he was rather elusive about it.

It worried her, but she was sure that his name would have preceded him, and Johann Strauss, whose music was to be heard everywhere, would at least welcome him as a fellow-artist.

In the meantime, *Frau* Bubna remembered him, and Gisela was determined to talk to her alone when the opportunity arose.

"You are doing well here," her father was saying. "Surely the place is a little larger than I remember?"

"Larger, *Mein Herr?* It is double the size!" *Frau* Bubna exclaimed. "We are fashionable. Everybody

3

sooner or later comes to drink my wines and eat my *Schnitzels.*"

"If they are as good as those we have had to-night," Paul Ferraris said, "then I am not surprised."

"Tomorrow I will cook you my *Palatschinken.*"

Paul Ferraris smiled with delight.

"No-one could cook them like you, *Mein Frau,* and I have already told my daughter that nothing in the world could be more delicious."

Gisela knew that *Palatschinken* consisted of thin dessert pancakes rolled round honey, fruits, and other succulent tit-bits.

Not once but a dozen times on that long journey her father had described to her what they were like, and she had to admit that the *Schnitzels* had lived up to her expectations, and so had the *Apfelstrudel.*

"I will soon grow fat if we stay here too long," Gisela said.

"You think you would grow fat like me?" *Frau* Bubna asked. "That is unlikely! I never could fatten your father, though I never knew a student who ate so much and was always so hungry."

Her father was still very thin, Gisela thought, and it made him look very elegant in his evening-clothes when he stood in the centre of the stage and lifted his precious Stradivarius violin and tucked it under his chin.

She had often thought that perhaps the ladies in the audience were as thrilled by him as they were by his music, and certainly their eyes were on his handsome face with his swept-back hair which was just beginning to turn grey at the temples.

"I am jealous of the attention you receive from such lovely ladies," her mother had said once.

"There is no need, my darling," her father had replied. "The only lovely lady in my life is you."

What was more, unlike most other musicians, her father's whole happiness was concentrated in his home.

4

He rarely went out to supper after a performance, which those who wanted to lionise him could not understand.

Instead he would drive back to wherever they were staying to have supper alone with his wife and later, when she grew older, with his daughter Gisela.

When her mother died, Gisela knew that her father would be lost, bewildered, and unhappy.

To see someone locked in the depths of despair was frightening, but she loved her father so much that she knew that for his sake, as well as for her mother's, she had to lift him out of his depression, and the only thing that could do that was music.

'Everything will be better now that he has come to Vienna,' she thought as she watched him talking animatedly with *Frau* Bubna.

At the same time, she knew by the lines under his eyes and the way he sometimes hesitated over a word that he was still tired.

As he finished his coffee with the thick cream floating on top of it, she said:

"Go to bed, Papa, and tomorrow, as there will be no horrible trains to catch and no pressing engagements to keep, you must sleep as late as you can."

"That is sensible," *Frau* Bubna agreed, "and you too, *Fraulein*, must have your beauty-sleep. *Gutennacht*, and God look over you!"

She went from the room as she spoke, and Gisela smiled at her father.

"She is wonderful!" she exclaimed. "I can understand why you wanted to see her again."

"She must be well over sixty," her father answered, "and yet she talks with the enthusiasm of a young girl and bounces round like a balloon!"

They both laughed.

"Tomorrow, when we are both properly awake," he said, "I will show you Vienna. I feel as if I have come home."

Gisela knew that in fact it was his adopted home,

but she did not say so, as it always annoyed her father to be reminded that he was half-English.

He had been unhappy living in England with his father, who she gathered was a strict martinet, and whose second wife resented Paul.

His grandparents on his mother's side had been Austrian and Paul had gone out to stay with them in the holidays. After they learnt how unhappy he was at home, they had kept him with them in Vienna.

They sent him to the University, and when they found that he had a great talent for music, especially for the violin, he had taken their name and made it his own.

"How can you possibly expect anyone to take you seriously as a musician if you are English?" his grandmother had said scornfully. "As Paul Ferraris they will listen to you with respect, and that is the first step in the battle for recognition."

Because he was an intelligent young man, Paul had known she was speaking good sense, and anyway he hated England and had no wish to be reminded of his unhappiness after his mother's death.

He soon thought of himself as belonging completely to her family, yet sometimes Gisela detected in her father English characteristics which he had no idea he possessed.

It was her mother who had insisted that wherever they went Gisela should work hard at her English lessons, as well as those in other languages.

"You are three-quarters English, my dearest," she said, "and it would be stupid to pretend otherwise. I have always believed that ultimately we all have our roots in the countries to which we belong, and perhaps one day you will go to England and find it is the place which appeals to you more than anywhere else."

"I think that is unlikely, Mama," Gisela replied, "but if you love England, I shall love it too. But Papa

6

has always made Austria sound so romantic and so exciting!"

"Your father conveniently forgets that he also has Hungarian blood in him, as his great-grandmother was Hungarian. So quite frankly, my dearest, he is a mongrel, although he is not prepared to admit it!"

They both laughed at this, but to Gisela it was very exciting that she could feel an affinity with the histories of England, Austria, Hungary, and, because they had lived there, France.

It also was easy for her to speak the languages of all four countries.

Being able to understand *Frau* Bubna, without having to mentally translate everything she said into another language, made her appreciate the hours she had spent with many different Governesses when she had longed to be out playing or riding in the sunshine.

'Tomorrow I shall listen to Austrian being spoken in the streets, in the shops, in the Restaurants, and of course in the Theatre,' she thought, 'and I shall also hear singing.'

She realised that that was what she had been missing since they had come to the Vienna Woods.

Her father had told her so often of how the students sang and the officers from the Barracks sang, and everybody would join in, their voices echoing and re-echoing amongst the trees.

Almost as if he knew what she was thinking, her father said suddenly:

"If I go to bed, Gisela, you must do the same. *Frau* Bubna is right. You need your beauty-sleep."

"It is very early, Papa."

"It is quiet tonight," her father replied, "unusually quiet. But *Frau* Bubna will have no time to look after you if people arrive for supper."

The way he said it made Gisela look at him in surprise.

7

"Do you mean they might be rowdy?" she asked.

Her father hesitated.

"Not exactly," he said. "For all I know it would be just good fun. But you are very lovely and are growing more like your mother every day. I am aware that at eighteen you should be chaperoned and can no longer run about freely like a child."

Gisela was surprised.

"This is something new, Papa! You have never talked to me like this before!"

"We have been living very quietly this past year," her father replied. "As you well know, we have not been to the cities that are gay, where beautiful women attract men's eyes like magnets."

"Do not worry about me, Papa," Gisela said. "I can look after myself. Anyway, we will talk about this tomorrow, not tonight."

She saw that his eyes were drooping with fatigue, and she knew that like all great artists he would one moment be pulsating with energy and vitality, and the next, almost as if the life-force had gone out of him, he would be limp to the point where she felt she must support him physically.

As if he knew that she was talking sense, Paul Ferraris rose to his feet, yawned, and walked towards the door.

"Goodnight, my dearest," he said. "You are as sensible as your mother always was. As you say, tomorrow we will talk, but not tonight."

He went from the room, which was a small private one at the back of the house where *Frau* Bubna had served their meal.

There was a Restaurant at the front of the Inn and a whole profusion of tables outside set in the shade of the trees, where Gisela had secretly looked forward to eating and watching the other diners.

But *Frau* Bubna had insisted that they have their meal early so that she could wait on them herself, and because both Paul Ferraris and Gisela felt extremely hungry, they were only too willing to agree.

Gisela picked up the soft wrap which matched her gown and which she had brought down with her in case she went out into the woods after dinner.

Now, instead of putting it round her shoulders, she draped it over one arm. Then she looked out the window and thought that, whatever her father might say, it was too early to go to bed.

She longed to have a closer look at the Vienna Woods, of which she had heard so much and read more.

She was also certain it would be the most romantic woods in the whole world, and what she had seen as they drove through it to the Inn had confirmed this impression.

The silver birches, the willows, the poplars, and the pussy-willows grew up and down the slopes. There were still a few lilacs left over from the early spring and a profusion of blossoms on trees and shrubs to which Gisela could not put names.

Almost as if she moved without thinking, she went out of the small room, and instead of climbing the twisting wooden stairs up to the next floor she walked through an open door that led into what might be termed the garden at the back of the house.

It was only a plot, thick with flowers that scented the air, then it became part of the woods, and the trees were so near that they seemed almost to be encroaching on the Inn.

Because it was so lovely and the night was not yet dark, Gisela walked on, and now as she moved beneath the heavy foliage above her and with the tree-trunks at her side, she could see below her the lights from the city of Vienna as they came on one by one.

There was not enough light to distinguish anything clearly except for the great spire of the Cathedral and the Danube, silver even in the dusk that was the prelude to darkness.

The lights of the city were like fallen stars and Gisela knew that when she could see through the foliage overhead, the stars in the sky would be coming out one by one to twinkle like diamonds against an iridescent background of the softest velvet.

It was exciting, and she felt as if she floated rather than walked over the ground.

Her feet were almost dancing in time to some celestial music which played in the leaves and in the flowers that she could smell even though she could not see them.

Then the trees on her left cleared a little and she could see the whole panorama of the Danube basin lying below her.

She knew that somewhere in the half-darkness there was Gansehaufel Island, and Korneuburg with its Castle, both of which she would be able to see tomorrow.

Her father had also promised to take her to look at the baroque Schönbrunn Palace, which was flanked by the domed Karlskirche.

There was so much to see, so much to hear, that it seemed almost a crime to think of sleep.

As more and more lights came on until it seemed as if the whole city was ablaze with them, she felt that she was missing something vital and exciting which was waiting there for her.

Perhaps, she told herself, that was what she expected of Vienna—that it would give her something she had always missed, although she was not quite certain what it was.

She knew only that because her father had talked about Vienna so often, it had an almost mystic meaning for her, but it was something she could not put into words and felt that instead it should be expressed in music.

It was then that she became aware that she was

hearing music, not the sort that her father played, but voices singing, men's voices.

She recognised the tune because ever since they had crossed the frontier into Austria they had heard it sung, whistled, and hummed, on the train, at every station at which they had stopped, and in every Inn in which they had stayed.

It was a popular waltz, and Gisela had soon learnt that the words changed and altered according to the needs of the singer.

Now as the voices came nearer and still nearer, she could hear them singing:

> *"I'm seeking love. Where is she hiding?*
> *I'm seeking love. Where can she be?*
> *Dancing, riding, singing or drinking,*
> *She will not escape me!"*

She had the feeling, although she was not quite sure, that these were the students' words they had made up to the music, and as they repeated the line: *"She will not escape me!"* they followed it with shouts that seemed quite literally to shake the leaves of the trees above her.

The voices were coming along the path on which she was standing, and she was suddenly aware how precarious her position was.

She had a feeling that the students might think it amusing to find a pretty girl alone in the woods.

She was sure they would not hurt her, but they might easily take it into their heads to kiss her and perhaps to force her to go along with them wherever they were going.

Suddenly panicking at the idea, Gisela wondered if she should run wildly back to the Inn.

But when she looked in the direction from which she had come, it was very dark under the trees, and she was afraid that if she hurried she might fall.

What was more, her white gown would be easily seen and might attract their attention.

11

She looked behind her and saw what she had not noticed before—a shelter or arbour that had been erected obviously for courting couples.

It contained a wooden seat, and there were shrubs and a vine overhead that had been trained to constitute some protection perhaps from the elements or perhaps from prying eyes.

Swiftly, because the men's voices were growing louder every moment, Gisela slipped into the arbour and, moving behind the seat, squeezed herself into the far corner.

Now as she listened she thought they did sound very jovial, as if they had already been imbibing the cheap beer that was so delicious or perhaps the local wine.

Her father had told her often that even the most impoverished student could afford a glass or two of Grinzing wine after a hard day in the University.

Because she was frightened, Gisela felt herself trembling as the voices came nearer, and now the words seemed to have an almost personal message for her.

> *"Dancing, riding, singing or drinking,*
> *She will not escape me!"*

'Supposing,' she thought, 'just supposing they notice me?'

She began to wish frantically that she had obeyed her father's instructions and gone to bed.

Of course she should not be alone in the woods at this time of the night, but it had all seemed so lovely, like a fantasy out of her imagination.

But this was reality, and young men were the same the world over.

Just as she was aware that the marching feet of the singers had reached the arbour and this was the dangerous moment when they might look in and see her gown, a splash of white against the shadows, a man appeared in the entrance.

Gisela's heart gave a leap of fear. Then she realised that he was not facing inwards but was standing with his back to her.

She could not see him clearly, but he was so tall that his head was level with the top of the arbour, and as he remained there she realised that since he was standing in that particular position, it would be impossible for the passing singers to look inside and see her.

After her first moment of fear at his appearance, she was grateful for him, and now the men's voices seemed almost deafening as they shouted: "*She will not escape me!*" and followed it with cheers and shouts of laughter.

The man in the entrance stood quite still as they passed by him, and she heard one of the singers say:

"Come and join us. The night is young and the wine at the Bubna Inn is good."

"I will do so later," the man replied.

The last of the singers moved away and the roar of their voices gradually receded until it was little more than a murmur in the distance.

Gisela realised that she had been holding her breath. Now she could breathe again, but she dared not move.

The man was still there and she wondered if he would follow the singers to the Inn as he had been asked to do.

Then as she realised that she was still trembling, although she was not as frightened as she had been at first, the man asked:

"You are all right?"

She had not realised that he knew she was there, and she started before she answered in a very small voice:

"Thank you for ... standing as you ... did. I was ... afraid they ... might see ... me."

"I thought that was why you were hiding," he

13

said. "It was a sensible thing to do, but it was not very sensible to come into the woods alone at night."

"I . . . know," Gisela replied, "but it was so . . . lovely and it . . . seemed almost . . . wrong to go to . . . bed."

She thought the man smiled, but she could not see his face for the night seemed to have grown much darker in the last few minutes, so that his body was only a blur against a very little light in the background.

"Who are you?" the man asked. "And why are you here?"

"I am staying with my father at the Inn. We only arrived today."

"I should imagine this is your first visit to Vienna."

"Why should you say that?"

"No-one who knows the city or the Viennese would come here alone."

Gisela gave a little sigh.

"It was very . . . foolish of me."

"Very! And something you must not do again."

There was a concerned note in his voice, which surprised her, and she looked at him enquiringly.

He must have sensed her curiosity, and he said:

"Come and sit down. I think it would be wise to allow those riotous young men to settle themselves before I take you back."

There was a pause, then Gisela said:

"You are . . . very kind."

She was not quite certain what she should do. She had the feeling that she should not be talking to a stranger, but the alternative was to walk away alone and she was too frightened to do that.

Because it seemed stupid not to do what he asked, she sat down on the seat and he sat beside her.

She realised that he was adult from the depth of

14

his voice, but he also seemed lithe and athletic from the way he moved.

It was impossible to be sure of anything else, and after a moment Gisela said nervously:

"I must go ... back as soon as ... you think it is ... safe."

"You will be safe with me."

She glanced at him quickly. Then, because she could see nothing in the darkness of the arbour, she looked out to where, even sitting down, she could see some of the lights in the city below.

"Suppose we introduce ourselves?" the man beside her suggested. "What is your name?"

"Gisela."

"A very pretty name, and I suspect you look like it."

Gisela could not help smiling.

"As you cannot see me," she said, "even if I were extremely ugly there would be no need for me to admit it."

"I am quite certain that you are beautiful."

Gisela laughed.

"How can you possibly be certain of that?"

"Because your voice is very musical and your figure is perfect."

She blushed and was glad it was too dark for him to notice.

"That is entirely ... supposition," she said, "and something you ... cannot prove."

"On the contrary," he replied. "I saw you standing against the sky when I came through the trees, and I thought you must be one of the nymphs who we all know live in these woods."

"I would love to see them!" Gisela exclaimed involuntarily.

The man beside her gave a little laugh.

"I have been fortunate enough to do so."

There was silence until Gisela said:

"I have told you my name . . . but what is . . . yours?"

"You told me half your name," he corrected. "Mine is Miklós."

"I am Gisela Ferraris."

The man at her side turned his head towards her.

"You are a relation of the musician?"

"You have heard of Papa?"

"Are you telling me that your father is Paul Ferraris, the violinist?"

"Yes."

"I heard him play last when I was in Paris, four or five years ago, and I have never forgotten how magnificent he was!"

Gisela clasped her hands together with a little cry.

"I am so glad! You must tell him that. He would be so pleased."

"I have always thought I would like to hear him again."

"Now will you tell me your name?" Gisela asked a little shyly.

"I am Miklós Toldi."

Gisela thought for a moment.

"That is not an Austrian name."

"No. I am Hungarian."

"How exciting!"

"Why should you think it is exciting?"

"I have always longed to meet a Hungarian. I have a little, a very little, Hungarian blood in my veins, and they always seem to me such a romantic race. More so than the Viennese, who Papa thinks are the most romantic people on earth."

"Perhaps your father is right. We all come to Vienna to talk, to dream, and to sing of love."

"Like the students," Gisela said with a little smile.

"The students are a lot of noisy, often tiresome young men," Miklós Toldi said, "and as they are often

16

unpredictable in their behaviour, it was very sensible
of you to hide when you heard them coming."

Gisela felt again that tremor of fear which had
passed through her when she knew that the singers
were encroaching on where she was hiding.

"Thank you for . . . saving me."

"I have already told you, you must be much more
sensible in the future, and I shall tell your father
when I meet him that he must look after you far more
strictly."

Gisela gave a cry of protest.

"You must do nothing of the sort! It would worry
and upset Papa, and it was only because I . . . dis-
obeyed him tonight that I am . . . here."

"Shall I say that as far as I am concerned I am
very glad you are," Miklós Toldi said. "At least we
have met, and I will not speak to your father about
you. Instead I will tell him he has a daughter whose
voice is more melodious than any sound he can produce on his violin."

Gisela laughed.

"Papa would not be complimented. Like all great
musicians, to him music is . . . sacred."

"He is right," Miklós Toldi said. "Your father is a
great musician and I shall certainly take the opportunity of hearing him again while I am in Vienna.
Where is he playing?"

Gisela made a helpless gesture with her hands.

"We only arrived . . . today," she said after a moment, "and there is so much I have to find out. Papa
must give a Concert or appear at a Theatre, but I do
not know . . . quite how to . . . arrange it."

"Are you saying that you arrange his performances?" Miklós Toldi asked incredulously.

"Ever since Mama died. He is helpless at anything like that, and because we have moved about so
much this last year when he has been so unhappy, he
has not got an Agent or a Manager as we had when
we were living in Paris."

"I understand," Miklós Toldi said. "I am sure if you go to see the Manager of the Court Theatre he will be delighted to help you."

"Thank you," Gisela said. "That is what I wanted to know. Papa is so vague about that sort of thing, and he would be just as happy playing in one of the small Wine-gardens, which he told me about, as playing to a smart audience in the Theatre."

She paused, then she added with a smile:

"Only, unfortunately, he would not be paid so well."

"You are in need of money?"

"We had to leave France in a hurry after the Germans had beaten the French at the Battle of Sedan. Since then we have been wandering in different parts of Europe, and travelling always costs money."

"I can see you are very practical, *Fraulein*, and just the sort of daughter your father should have."

"I try to be," Gisela said, "but he will not always listen to me as he did to Mama."

"Of course not. People, especially men, expect their children to obey, not to give them orders."

"That is true," Gisela agreed, "but I can usually coax Papa into doing what I want."

"What woman has not the wiles of Eve at her finger-tips to get her own way?" Miklós Toldi asked almost cynically.

Because she felt that he was criticising her, Gisela rose to her feet.

"There is no sound now from the direction of the Inn," she said, "and I feel sure it would be safe for me to go back."

Miklós Toldi rose too.

"I will take you back."

"There is no need."

"You cannot be sure of that. The students might return this way."

18

He knew by the way she instinctively looked in the direction of the Inn that the idea made her nervous, and he said quietly:

"Unless you know the way, it is not easy to find the Inn even in daylight. Give me your hand and I will lead you."

Gisela hesitated for a moment, then she thought it would seem very foolish if she refused what was an eminently sensible suggestion.

She put out her hand and felt his fingers close over hers.

They were warm and strong and very reassuring.

Then they set off side by side along the path by which she had walked from the Inn.

She realised that he was right when he said it would be difficult to find.

When they had their backs to the lights from the city, they moved straight into the darkness of the wood.

The trees overhead were so thick that there was no sign of the stars, and tonight there was no moon.

As he clasped her hand Gisela stumbled and he held her steady, his fingers tightening on hers, and she was glad that he was with her.

They walked in silence until at last, looming ahead of them like a beacon, there were the lights of the Inn.

"I am safe now!" Gisela exclaimed when they had almost reached the small garden.

Still in the shadow of the trees, Miklós stopped, and as he was still holding her hand she was obliged to stop too.

"I have brought you back safely, Gisela," he said.

She was surprised that he used her Christian name, but she did not say anything, and he went on:

"I doubt if we shall meet again, because I have remembered that I have to leave Vienna tomorrow."

"You will go away without seeing Papa? But I thought you said you wanted to hear him play?"

"I do want to hear him," Miklós Toldi said, "but I have personal and pressing reasons for leaving and it will therefore be impossible."

"I am sorry. Papa would have been so pleased to talk to you about Paris."

"Perhaps another time," he said. "But I know what I will do. I will speak to the Manager of the Court Theatre before I leave and tell him that you will be calling on him tomorrow with your father."

"That is very kind of you."

"I happen to know him, and I will make sure that he helps you in one way or another."

"Thank you! Thank you!" Gisela cried. "That will make everything very much easier for us. You are so kind, and I was so lucky that you were there tonight to save me."

"In the future, take great care of yourself. Another time I will not be there, and you might be really frightened."

He paused before he said:

"Promise me you will take no risks."

There was something very serious in his voice, and she lifted her face up to his, trying to see in the darkness what he looked like.

She could only see that he was taller than she was, and as the lights from the Inn did not reach the trees, he was just a voice in the dark.

"Promise me," Miklós Toldi insisted.

"I promise," Gisela answered.

"I shall remember your voice, just as I shall remember your father's music."

"You know how very grateful I am," she said impulsively. "I wish I could thank you more ... adequately."

"That is easy," Miklós replied.

Gisela looked at him, puzzled, not understanding what he was saying.

Then very gently, as if he was afraid of frightening her, his arm went round her, and with his other hand he tipped her face up to his.

For a moment she was too surprised to move. Then as she attempted to do so, it was too late.

His lips came down on hers and she received the first kiss she had ever had in her life.

She knew she ought to struggle, and somewhere far away at the back of her mind she thought she should be angry.

Miklós Toldi's arms held her close against him, his mouth held her captive, and it was impossible to move, impossible even to think.

She knew only that his lips seemed first to take her prisoner, then something warm and wonderful like a wave from the sea moved within her and flooded up through her breasts and into her throat until it touched her lips.

It was so lovely that it was part of the music she had heard in the trees, part too of the lights of the city, looking like fallen stars, and part of the silver of the river and of the fragrance of the flowers in the garden.

It was something she had dreamt of, imagined, thought she would never find, yet it was what she had expected of Vienna, and now it was hers.

His arms tightened and his lips became a little more demanding and more insistent, and yet he was still gentle so that she was not afraid.

She felt that she had ceased to exist and was no longer herself but a part of him.

He kissed her until she felt as if her feet no longer were on the ground and they were both flying up into the sky and were part of the stars.

Then when it seemed to Gisela that it was impossible to feel such rapture and not die at the wonder of it, he raised his head.

"Good-bye," he said, and his voice was hoarse and very unlike what it had been before.

She wanted to beg him not to go, but it was impossible to speak, and when she could do so he was gone.

One moment he had been there in the darkness, holding her in his arms, and the next he had vanished between the tree-trunks and she was alone.

It was only then that Gisela came back to reality and it all seemed to have been a dream.

Had she really gone into the Vienna Woods and been frightened by the students? Had she really been saved by a man whose face she had never seen, and whom reprehensibly and in fact shockingly she had allowed to kiss her? But there had been a rightness about it, or perhaps the proper word was "inevitability." It was what she had expected of Vienna, and what she had found.

Then she realised that he had gone, he had said good-bye, and she would never see him again.

Not that she had seen him in actual fact, but she knew that in a strange, unaccountable way she had responded to his voice and to the touch of his hand.

She could still feel his fingers holding hers, keeping her safe and secure in the darkness of the woods.

Her heart was beating and her whole body was throbbing with the ecstasy he had aroused in her with his lips, and she thought it could never be possible for her ever again to feel as she had when he was holding her captive.

A rapture which she could not explain had moved upwards within her to make her part of him.

Then he had left her, and she thought there was only the lingering note of his voice on the air, saying "good-bye."

Because it seemed so unreal, something which could not have happened, she turned round blindly to move slowly, almost as if she were sleep-walking, through the flower-filled garden back into the Inn.

She walked along the passage and as she reached the staircase she could hear the chatter and laughter of voices in the Restaurant and outside under the trees.

Because she was afraid that she might meet somebody and have to speak to them, Gisela hurried up the stairs.

Only as she reached the door of her own bedroom did she hear faintly the sound of voices coming from the garden:

"I'm seeking love. Where is she hiding?
I'm seeking love. Where can she be?"

Chapter Two

In a box, watching a rehearsal taking place on the stage, Gisela with a feeling of satisfaction thought that it was going very well.

She had felt a little apprehensive as she and her father were driving into the city to see the Manager of the Court Theatre.

She obviously could not tell her father that Miklós Toldi had said that he would speak to the Manager, because in no way could she explain her acquaintanceship with a man whom he had never heard of before.

Besides, Gisela was quite certain that she would not be able to speak of the man who had kissed her without blushing.

After she had lain awake the first night, still feeling the rapture and wonder that he had evoked in her with his lips, it had been impossible to have any regrets or even recriminations.

But the following morning she had been ashamed and shocked at herself.

How could she have behaved in such a fast, loose manner?

She was well aware that her mother would have been horrified at the idea of her being kissed by any man to whom she was not engaged to be married.

But for a stranger, a man whose face she had not even seen, to kiss her in the Vienna Woods seemed in

24

retrospect so incredible, so completely unbelievable, that Gisela kept telling herself that it had not really happened but was just a figment of her imagination.

But when she tried to do so she could feel Miklós Toldi's arms round her and his lips on hers.

She could hear again the music playing in the leaves of the trees and experience again the feeling that she was being swept up towards the stars, and the ecstasy of it was almost too wonderful to be borne.

When she breakfasted very late with her father under the trees outside the Inn, she told herself severely that she had to come down to earth and think only of him.

He still looked tired, but he was as enthusiastic as a young boy at the idea of showing her Vienna and finding some of his friends.

"I may call on Johannes Brahms," he said. "*Frau* Bubna has told me his address."

"I think first, Papa," Gisela answered, "we should visit the Manager of one of the Theatres who might offer you a Concert or a place in one of his Shows."

"They will all want me," her father replied quickly.

But it was too quickly for Gisela not to realise that he was, if he was truthful, a little apprehensive that he might not receive the welcome he hoped for.

Thanks, she was sure, to Miklós Toldi, when they arrived at the Court Theatre they were ushered immediately and with much ceremony into the Manager's office.

He was an elderly man, fat and bald, and he rose from his desk with an unmistakable cry of delight.

"*Herr* Ferraris!" he exclaimed. "I can hardly believe it is you! But welcome, welcome to the City of Music!"

"You have heard of my success in Paris?" Paul Ferraris asked.

"Of course, and we now need you among us!"

From that moment everything went smoothly, and within two days Paul Ferraris was attending rehearsals for a Show which was to open at the end of the week.

"We need you desperately," the Producer told him. "We have a great baritone, Ferdinand Jaeger, and a violin solo will be a delightful contrast, an item which is at the moment missing from the programme."

Paul Ferraris had been thrilled.

"They have heard of me! I told you they would!"

"But of course, Papa," Gisela said. "Music is international, and I cannot believe that Vienna has been out-of-touch with Paris and Brussels all these years."

Sitting now far back in the box so that she could not be seen either from the stage or from the Auditorium, Gisela said a little prayer of thanks because her father looked so happy.

She knew from the way he walked onto the stage that he would play his best and forget the frustrations of the last year when he had often been too unhappy to do so.

He had always been very particular that Gisela should not associate with the Theatre people, who, although he did not say so, often had morals of which he disapproved.

When her mother was alive, Gisela had always been left at home, and the few times when she went to the Theatre, it was to sit in a box or the stalls to listen to her father, and never to go back-stage to see him.

Now Paul Ferraris was worried about what to do with her.

He obviously could not order her to stay alone in the Hotel where they were staying, and to let her sit in the stalls with the Director and other people concerned with the production would mean that she would be mixing with them in a way that he considered undesirable.

"They are all performers like yourself," Gisela argued, "and I want to meet them."

"Your mother would not approve," her father replied firmly, "but leave everything to me. I will make the arrangements I think best."

Gisela had no wish to argue with him.

But she felt that if she was not there, he would not look after himself and would forget to have anything to eat when he should do so, or in the excitement of meeting old friends would forget to return to the Hotel.

When they reached the Theatre her father had a talk with the Manager which resulted in her being shown into one of the private boxes at the back of the Auditorium and shut in, Gisela told herself with a wry smile, as if she were a wild animal.

She did not wish to complain, and it was fascinating to see the Court Theatre, which looked to her very beautiful, even though she was told that a new one was being built as this was not considered grand enough as the Imperial Theatre of the Capital.

The Opera-House had been constructed several years later and was the first public building on the Ring.

Gisela longed to visit it, but for the moment there was no time for sight-seeing as her father insisted on rehearsing every possible minute of the day.

"I am rusty and out of practice," he said, "and if I am to appear in front of the most critical musical audience in the world, I shall have to work day and night, if necessary, to preserve my reputation."

"You play beautifully, Papa!"

However, Gisela could understand his being a little nervous, for she had already learnt that the Viennese talked and thought of little but music, and when they were not playing they sang.

27

Now she was listening to the Orchestra and she thought her father was right in saying that music in Vienna achieved a perfection which was not to be found anywhere else.

The Orchestra finished and someone sitting in the stalls called out:

"Paul Ferraris!"

Her father walked onto the stage.

Even in his ordinary day-clothes which he wore for rehearsals he looked, Gisela thought, more distinguished and more handsome than any other man in the Theatre.

He might wish to think of himself as Austrian, but there was an authoritative air about him which she was sure was due to his English blood.

"Englishmen are always aware of their own consequence," her mother had said to her with a smile, "and as at the moment they have an unassailable position in the world, I am very proud, whatever your father may say, that he and I, and you, my darling, are English."

"You must not say so to him!" Gisela had said in a warning voice.

They had both laughed, knowing how fervently Paul Ferraris tried to prove that he was completely Austrian in thought, word, and deed.

Now he stood for a moment looking round the Theatre almost as if it were filled with an audience waiting breathlessly to hear what he had to say to them.

Then he lifted his beloved Stradivarius, and Gisela thought proudly that no girl could have a more wonderful father.

He tucked his silk handkerchief under his chin, the Conductor of the Orchestra raised his baton, and the exquisite strains of one of Mozart's Concertos filled the air.

It was so lovely that Gisela felt that she was not

in the Theatre but in the Vienna Woods, with the lights of the city twinkling below, the stars bright in the night sky, the music coming not from the stage but from the leaves of the trees overhead.

Because she was in the woods it was impossible for her not to feel that Miklós was with her and that the touch of his hand gave her a feeling of safety and security.

Then his arms were round her and his lips on hers!

She was so intent on her thoughts that it was not until Gisela heard her father finish the first item of his programme and pause before he started the next that she came from her world of fantasy back to reality and realised that she was not alone in the box.

Somebody was sitting beside her, and because she thought it must be the Manager she turned towards him, ready to hear him praise her father's performance. But to her astonishment it was a man she had never seen before.

Then as she looked at him and saw his eyes looking intently at her, she knew, before he spoke and before there was any need for an explanation, who he was.

"You are just as I expected you to look," he said.

His voice was deep and familiar and had been ringing in her ears ever since they had talked in the dark.

"Why . . . are you . . . here?" she asked. "I thought . . . you said you were . . . going away."

"I tried to do so," he replied, "and I want to tell you about it. When can I see you alone?"

She stared at him in perplexity. Then she said:

"I know I have to . . . thank you for telling the Manager that Papa was . . . coming, and he has been . . . very kind."

"There is no reason why he should not be,"

29

Miklós Toldi replied. "At the same time, a surprise appearance does not always work out the way one would want."

"I am very ... grateful."

"You are always very generous with your thanks."

Gisela blushed as she remembered how she had tried to thank him and he had kissed her.

"You are lovely!" he exclaimed. "And more lovely than anyone I have ever seen when you blush."

"Please ..." Gisela pleaded, "you are ... making me feel ... shy."

"And that is as beautiful as your voice," he said. "Answer my question, because if you have not told your father we have already met, he may think it strange that we are sitting here talking to each other."

Gisela started and moved a little farther towards the back of the box, where she was hidden by the fringed red velvet curtains which hung on either side of it.

"Please ... do not let him see you," she pleaded.

"Then answer my question," he replied.

Gisela glanced nervously at the stage.

Her father was playing again, and now it was one of his favourite pieces written by Schubert.

"It is impossible for us to do so!" she whispered. "Papa never lets me out of his sight except when he is performing, and he will not leave me alone at the Hotel."

"I have to see you," Miklós Toldi said urgently, "and you have told me that you are grateful."

"I think you are ... blackmailing ... me," Gisela protested.

"Only because I so desperately want to talk to you."

He gave a little sigh, then he said:

"I left Vienna as I told you I intended to do, and when I was a hundred miles away from the city I turned back."

"To see . . . me?"

"How could I leave unfinished a Symphony or a Concerto so beautiful, so inspiring, that it would be a crime against nature not to know the ending?"

He paused before he said:

"That is not the word I want, but you know what I am trying to say."

"I . . . cannot meet . . . you . . ."

Even as Gisela spoke the words she paused.

"What is it?" Miklós Toldi asked.

"I had . . . really forgotten . . . about it . . . and anyway . . . it would be . . . wrong."

"Not if it concerns you and me, so tell me what you have remembered."

"It is just that when we were coming here Papa told me that after the rehearsal this evening he is going to supper with Johann Strauss. He is very excited about it, as he had been so looking forward to seeing him, but he told me that I had not been invited and he would take me back to the Hotel first."

She knew without looking at him that Miklós Toldi was smiling.

Then he said:

"I suppose your father believes, as so many other people do, that Johann Strauss's melodies may please the aristocrats but would corrupt the young."

"No, no, of course not!" Gisela said. "How could he think anything so foolish when Mr. Strauss's music is so lovely?"

"Lovely and romantic to you and me," Miklós Toldi said quietly, "and I need not tell you how much I want to dance with you. But the more strait-laced Austrians say that the waltz is restless—passionate— and often that 'the Devil is loose.'"

Gisela gave a little laugh because it sounded to her so ridiculous.

Then she said:

"There are always people who disapprove of anything that is new and modern, but before the war everybody in Paris waltzed to Strauss's music and thought it a perfect compliment to the Empress Eugénie's beautiful gowns from Worth and her glittering jewels."

"You are too young to have waltzed in Paris."

"Yes, I know, and now it is all over," Gisela said wistfully, "but Mama used to tell me about the Balls, and she would take me to the Theatre when Papa was playing so I could see the Emperor and the Empress sitting in the Royal Box, and everybody in the audience looked as if they had stepped out of a fairytale."

"I am glad you were too young to waltz in Paris," Miklós Toldi remarked quickly.

"Why?" Gisela asked innocently.

"Because now you are old enough to waltz with me in Vienna," he replied.

For a moment the feeling of how wonderful that would be seeped into her mind. Then she said quickly:

"You know that is ... impossible. Papa would never ... allow it."

"We will argue about that later," Miklós Toldi said. "Tonight I want to talk to you somewhere quiet where we will not be seen."

"I cannot ... I must not do ... anything like ... that!"

"Please," he pleaded. "Please remember that I helped you once and might be able to do so again. And also that I have come back a hundred miles just to see you."

"I am sure you had ... other reasons," Gisela said defensively.

"No, just you," he said softly.

She tried to tell herself that what he was suggesting was wrong and that she could not possibly deceive her father or behave in a manner which would merely augment her outrageous behaviour in the woods.

Then as she looked at him to say the words which trembled on her lips, they seemed to fade away so that all she could think of was the expression in his eyes and how exceedingly handsome he was.

He did in fact look very different from any man she had ever seen before.

His hair, which was dark, was brushed back from a square forehead, his clear-cut features were unusual and so were his eyes, dark with a light that in a strange way seemed to make them compelling and yet somehow at the same time trustworthy.

She knew that with any other man she would have been extremely apprehensive at the suggestion which Miklós Toldi had made to her.

Yet, in the same way she had known that when he led her through the darkness she could trust and rely on him, she knew she could trust him now.

"You will come?"

She could barely hear the words, and yet they were like a kiss against her lips.

"You have been so . . . kind that it is . . . difficult to say 'no.'"

"You are only making excuses to yourself," he said. "You know that the real reason you will come is that you want to talk to me as much as I want to talk to you. We cannot escape each other, Gisela."

As he spoke he put out his hand, took hers, and raised it to his lips.

She felt his mouth warm and compelling against her skin, then he moved from the box just as her father played the last notes of Schubert's exquisite study for violin, and she was alone.

* * *

Travelling back to the Theatre that evening, Gisela found it hard to think of anything but what lay ahead.

Late in the afternoon they had gone back to the Sacher Hotel, where they were staying, and her father lay down and almost immediately went to sleep.

Gisela waited first to arrange that he should have something to eat and drink before they went back to the Theatre.

After a discussion with the Chef, who had assured her that he would do anything to make such a famous man as her father happy, she had walked through the narrow twisting passages upstairs to her room.

She found the Hotel fascinating, although she had been rather horrified when her father had insisted on staying there.

"Can we afford it, Papa?"

"There is nowhere else I would want to stay in Vienna," her father had said firmly.

She had not wanted to spoil his pleasure by saying that they should go to some cheap *Pension*.

The Sacher Hotel, which stood behind the Opera-House, was to Gisela very impressive, with oil-paintings, sculptures, and *objets d'art* that seemed to belong more to a private house than to an Hotel.

When they had arrived they had been greeted with the exquisite politeness that Gisela was beginning to find was very much part of Vienna.

Never had she imagined in all the years she had lived in other countries that such courtesy could be extended no less by a lovely member of Austrian society than by an aristocrat.

"I kiss your hand," a porter would say if she gave him a small tip. Or: "I lay myself at the gracious lady's feet," from the cab-driver as he set them down at the Theatre.

It all added to the glamour of the city, of which she had so far seen so very little and longed to see more.

"As soon as the rehearsals are over, my dearest," her father had said, "and I only have to be at the Theatre in the evening, I will begin to show you all the places I have loved and which to me are the most beautiful and of course the most romantic."

He smiled, as if he suspected that was what she was looking for, and she wondered guiltily what he would say if he knew that romance had come to her already in a very different way when she had least expected it.

Luckily the rehearsal was soon over, because while she was in a hurry for it to finish, she knew that her father was looking forward so much to his evening with Johann Strauss.

Even so, because she was nervous as well as excited, Gisela thought that the hours dragged by slowly until finally the Producer said in excited tone:

"That is enough for tonight. You were all magnificent, but there is still a great deal to be done. Ten o'clock tomorrow morning, and please, I beg of you not to be late or I shall throw myself into the Danube!"

There was laughter at this. Then as everyone trooped off the stage, Gisela waited in the box, as she had been told to do, until her father came to fetch her.

Most of the others had left by the stage door, but he had arranged with the Manager that the *fiacre* that would carry them back to their Hotel would be in the front of the building.

It was a very amusing little carriage that Gisela had never seen anywhere else.

Drawn by two horses, it was like two large perambulators put together with their collapsible hoods meeting in the middle.

She and her father stepped into it and sat facing each other, and the horses set off and drove through the streets bright with lights and filled with people who obviously had no intention of going to bed for many hours yet.

"The rehearsal went very well," Paul Ferraris said with satisfaction.

"You played better than I have ever heard you, Papa," Gisela said truthfully.

"I am beginning to get back into the spirit of it all," her father replied. "Vienna, as you know, inspires me, as it has inspired so many musicians in the past, and I feel they are all round us still; encouraging, applauding, and of course criticising."

Gisela laughed.

"That must be very intimidating. I would hate to think that Gluck and Haydn might be saying you could do better, or that Mozart and Beethoven are wishing you would interpret their music in a different way."

"They might, on the other hand, think I have improved it," Paul Ferraris said.

"Now you are being conceited, Papa, and it is because of all the compliments you have received here."

"I am enjoying every one of them!"

Because he looked so happy, Gisela thought thankfully that at least he was beginning to get over her mother's death.

The horses drew up outside the Sacher Hotel and Paul Ferraris bent forward to kiss his daughter on the cheek.

"Good-night, my dearest. I am sorry you cannot accompany me. One day I may perhaps allow you to meet Johann Strauss, but at the moment I would rather you lost your heart to his music than to him!"

"Good-night, Papa," Gisela said with a smile, as she stood on the pavement.

As the carriage drove away, she walked into the Hotel.

She had already decided that she would go up to her bedroom and wait until she was told that somebody had called for her.

Then, if she behaved properly, she would make her excuses and send him away, but she knew that instead she would go out to supper with Miklós, not only because she was grateful but because there was something about him that was irresistible.

She walked towards the staircase, and as she did so, one of the porters came up to her to say:

"Excuse me, gracious *Fraulein,* but there is a gentleman waiting for you."

Gisela started and looked round.

"This way, *Fraulein.*"

She followed the porter to the door of a Sitting-Room which she had not previously entered.

It was small, and there was no-one there except for one person, and she felt her heart leap at the sight of him.

He was tall, as she had guessed the first time she had seen him silhouetted against the sky, when he had stood protectively in the entrance to the arbour where she was hiding.

She realised that looking at him in the box at the Theatre was not the same as seeing him dressed in evening-clothes and standing with his back to the fireplace.

There was something magnificent about him, and she was instantly conscious that her gown, although it was a very pretty one, somehow did not measure up to his standard.

Almost as if he read her thoughts, Miklós Toldi said:

"I told you you were lovely when I saw you in the shadows of the arbour, but now I see that was an understatement."

Gisela's eyes fell before his, and she blushed.

Then as she walked towards him he said:

"I am now quite certain that you really are a nymph from the Vienna Woods, as I first thought you to be."

She found it impossible to know what to say, and after a moment Miklós went on:

"Just in case your father should learn on his return that you have gone out, I have arranged for us to leave the Hotel by a different door."

"Thank you," Gisela said.

She was vividly conscious of him as they walked together across the room and he escorted her down the passage which led to the side of the Hotel where there was a door onto a different street.

A porter was waiting to open it for them and Miklós tipped him and he expressed his gratitude in the usual fulsome manner.

When she went outside Gisela saw that there was a very impressive carriage waiting, drawn by two horses with a coachman to drive them and a footman to open the door for them.

She had the feeling that it was not a hired carriage, and again, as if he knew what she was thinking, Miklós said with a smile:

"If you are curious, I have borrowed this conveyance for this evening."

"It is certainly very comfortable," Gisela said in a small voice, leaning back against the heavily padded seat.

"I am glad you think so," Miklós said, "because I am taking you a little way out of Vienna."

"Where to?"

"Somewhere I am quite certain you have heard of, even if you have not had time to visit it."

"And where is that?"

"Grinzing."

"Papa has told me about it, and I know it is where the Wine-gardens are."

"Exactly!" Miklós said, "and I want to be the first to take you to them."

"It will be very . . . exciting for me."

"And for me," he added quietly.

The horses moved swiftly, and because Gisela found it difficult to make conversation when she was aware that Miklós was sitting sideways looking at her, they drove almost in silence.

The lights in the streets and the windows as they passed seemed, as they flashed by, to illuminate the inside of the carriage for a moment and then be gone, so that it was a matter of light and dark, light and dark.

This in itself brought another excitement to Gisela, who was already aware that because she was doing something she ought not to do, she felt different and unlike herself.

Always before in her life she had been scrupulously well behaved because she had wished to do nothing else but obey her mother and father, and, because she loved them and they loved her, there could be no question of her doing anything else.

Now, in some strange manner, a man she had only met twice before was turning her whole world upside-down and she was not certain what she felt about it, except that it was exciting.

The horses first took them away from the houses, then they were outside the city and climbing up the lower slope of a hill, where she knew if it were light enough she could have seen the famous vines her father had told her about.

He had described how the white wine from them was drunk in the local *Heuriger* Taverns when the season arrived.

"Each Tavern, when it has pressed its own new wine," he had explained, "hangs out on a pole a wreath of evergreens as a token sign that the wine is now ready."

As Gisela remembered what he had said, the horses came to a standstill in a quiet street and she thought she had made a mistake

But Miklós helped her alight, then opened a door of an Eighteenth-Century, one-storey house, and she found herself in a garden.

In the back across the garden there was a Tavern decorated with colourful murals and window-boxes brilliant with flowers.

In the garden there were long, small tables and round them were small, intimate alcoves covered over with vines.

The Proprietor, who obviously knew Miklós, bowed low at the sight of him and exclaimed with delight that he should honour them once again with his presence.

Then he led the way to an alcove that seemed more profusely covered with vines than any of the others and was in a quiet corner of the garden, away from the other people present.

Inside was a table and two comfortably cushioned chairs which were set close to each other so that Gisela and Miklós sat side by side rather than facing.

"Papa has described these Taverns to me so often," Gisela said, "and it is what I have always longed to see."

"Here you can drink the thin white wine of Grinzing," Miklós said, "and I promise you the food is delicious!"

Gisela was sure it was, but afterwards, although she knew she had eaten, she could never remember what it tasted like.

This was because she could listen to Miklós's deep voice talking to her and he was very near, so near that she could almost feel the vibrations from him.

The meal came to end and he said:

"Now we can talk, and I can look at you, Gisela, although I am still afraid you may vanish into the trees and I shall be left alone."

"I will not do that, and it was you who vanished! One moment you were there, and the next you had . . . gone!"

"And what did you feel?"

It was impossible to find the words to answer him. So she said:

"I . . . I do not think we should talk about it."

"But I want to know," he insisted. "I want to know what you thought after I had kissed you, and I know it was the first time you had ever been kissed."

"How . . . how could you . . . know that?"

He smiled.

"Your lips were very young, sweet, and innocent."

As he spoke he watched the colour that crept up her cheeks, and said:

"And, my dear, I had forgotten that a woman could blush so adorably, or look so breathtakingly and entrancingly young."

The way he spoke made Gisela feel that her heart was doing very strange things in her breast.

It was almost a relief when at that moment more wine was brought to their table and poured out.

She felt as if she had time to breathe before they were alone again.

Miklós raised his glass.

"To my nymph from the Vienna Woods, from whom I could not escape!" he said.

Gisela looked at him in a puzzled way.

"Why did you want to escape?"

She knew by the expression on his face that she had asked him an important question, although she had no idea why it should be so.

"That is something I should explain to you," he said, "but not now. Later this evening. The night is still young."

They talked not about themselves but about music, the stage, and the parts of the world to which Gisela had been with her father.

"I wish I could say that I have been to your country," she said.

"I am glad you have not."

"Why?"

"Because if you had, I could not show it to you myself. You told me that you have a little Hungarian blood in your veins. How is that?"

"My father's great-grandmother was Hungarian, and she is therefore my great-great-grandmother."

"Even one drop of Hungarian blood is better than

none," Miklós said with a smile. "What was your great-great-grandmother's name?"

"Rákoczl."

"The Rákoczls are a revered and very important family in Hungary."

"I am glad about that. Papa has always said that the red lights in my hair come from my great-great-grandmother."

Miklós looked at her hair.

It was a very deep gold with little flames touching the curls which Gisela always had trouble in keeping tidy.

Her hair seemed somehow to have a life of its own, and however hard she brushed and combed it into place, it would escape in little tendrils round her cheeks, or rise as if drawn by fairy-fingers above her head.

Miklós's eyes flickered over it now.

"Like everything else about you," he said, "your hair is beautiful and also unique."

"I am pleased that I do not . . . look like . . . everybody else! At the same time, I am told that Vienna is full of beautiful women."

"That is true, but I promised you would shine amongst them, and I would like to have seen you doing so."

He spoke as if it was something he would not be there to see, and after a moment Gisela asked in a low voice:

"Are you . . . going away . . . again?"

"I should not have come back."

He spoke so sharply that she looked at him in surprise, and after a moment he said:

"Oh, my dear, if you think you are behaving badly, it is nothing to what I am doing! I tried to do the right thing. I tried to go away, but I had to return to find out if you were real—that I had not dreamt that moment of rapture when I touched your lips!"

This was what she had thought herself, and because of the way he spoke, Gisela felt her heart turn over in her breast.

Then she clasped her hands together as if to stop herself from trembling.

After a moment she said almost inaudibly:

"Why ... is ... what you are doing ... wrong?"

There was a long silence, so long that Gisela could feel her heart beating almost as if it were trying to escape from her.

Then when Miklós did not answer her, suddenly the music being played by the Tavern's *Schrammel* quartet at the far end of the garden burst into a Strauss waltz.

There was a terrace outside the Inn, and the musicians, consisting of first and second violins, a guitar, and an accordion, were sitting at one side of it, and as soon as they started the waltz one or two couples left their tables and began to dance.

Gisela looked at them casually, but she felt too bemused by what Miklós was saying to be really interested.

Then unexpectedly he rose from the table and taking her hand drew her to her feet.

"Your first waltz in Vienna," he said, "and it was meant to be with me."

He smiled at her and her fingers tightened on his.

"I hope I dance ... well enough."

"I am not afraid that you will disappoint me."

They walked through the tables and onto the terrace.

Most people were still eating and drinking, and there was plenty of room for Miklós to swing Gisela round to the alluring strains of the waltz, which seemed to lift both the heart and the mind and infuse them with a gaiety which was almost like the golden wine they had just drunk.

43

Round and round they went, and Gisela was acutely conscious of his arm round her waist and her hand in his, and that she was very close to him.

When he looked down at her she could see his lips, and she remembered how they had held her captive and the ecstasy that they had given her.

Suddenly, as they seemed to fly over the ground rather than dance, she knew that what she felt for Miklós was love.

It was love mixed with the excitement of the night, with her courage in coming here alone with him, and with the thrill of dancing.

He was the most attractive man she had ever seen. But it was much more than that.

There was some strange link between her and Miklós that had vibrated from him from the moment he had protected her in the woods, and which had grown and intensified until at this moment it was a part of the beat of her heart and of the very air she breathed.

She knew, as his arm tightened and he swung her quicker and still quicker to the tempo of the waltz, that this was love.

The love she had always believed would come to her, but not for a man who had come into her life in the darkness and who, she had the frightening feeling, would at any moment vanish for the second time.

Chapter Three

"I think I should go home."

It was hard to say the words. The evening seemed to have flown by on wings, but Gisela was certain it was getting late, and she wondered what would happen if her father wanted her and found that she was not in her bedroom.

It was unlikely, but while every moment with Miklós had been glorious, there was a touch of a guilty conscience nagging away at the back of her mind.

"You are right," Miklós said. "At the same time, it is hard, desperately hard, to let you go."

There was silence, and Gisela waited for him to say that perhaps they could meet another night.

Then, as he did not do so, she could not help looking at him enquiringly.

"I know what you are thinking," he said in a low voice, "but I have to leave and drive away as I did before—but this time I must not come back."

"But . . . why?" Gisela asked.

He looked at her and she thought there was an expression of pain in his eyes, but she could not be certain.

She knew only that the evening had been an enchantment that she still could not believe was real because it seemed a romantic, glamorous, and glorious episode which she had dreamt.

"There is so much I should say to you," Miklós said, "instead of which I just want to go on telling you how beautiful you are, and how from the moment I saw you silhouetted against the sky I knew that you could mean something in my life that until then had been missing, although I was not certain what it was."

"How could you ... possibly know ... that?" Gisela asked.

He smiled and said:

"I think we are both aware that something links us as it does not do with other people. I knew it when I saw you, I was sure of it when I talked to you and when I touched your lips. Then I was aware that I had found the ideal woman who had always been hidden in a shrine in my heart."

Gisela looked at him, and because his words made her feel as if the sunlight enveloped them, she began to tremble.

Suddenly, so unexpectedly that it made her start, Miklós rose to his feet, pushing away the table and saying in a harsh voice that seemed to destroy the enchantment of the night:

"Come! We must leave. I will take you back."

Wide-eyed with surprise and at the same time hurt by the way he had spoken to her, Gisela also rose.

Then as Miklós, having thrown down on the table what seemed an enormous amount of money, moved towards the entrance of the arbour, the Orchestra started to play a tune they both recognised.

It was the song which had brought them together, the song which had warned Gisela that she was in danger, from which Miklós had saved her.

As if he too remembered what it meant to both of them, he turned to look at her, and at that moment a woman's voice, soft, with a clear, lovely soprano, started to sing the original words which the students had parodied:

"I'm seeking love, where is he hiding?
I'm seeking love, where can he be?"

Miklós held out his hand, and as Gisela took it he drew her through the garden once more and onto the terrace.

Then they were dancing and the song went on:

"High in the sky a rainbow riding
Whispers a secret to me:
'Rest assured love will find you
Know that he is very near.'
I'm seeking love, is he behind you?
I'm seeking love. O!—he is here!"

At the last words Gisela looked up into Miklós's eyes, and as he swung her round he said very softly:

"I think my lovely one, that neither of us can deny that we have found love."

His arm tightened and there was no need for Gisela to reply.

They were close not only with their bodies but with their minds and their hearts. They did not speak again.

When the waltz ended they walked, still in silence, out of the garden to where the carriage was waiting.

It must have been at Miklós's orders that the hood had been folded back, and after the footman had put a light rug over their knees, he drew closer to Gisela and took her hand in his.

Then they were driving back towards the city under the stars which seemed to fill the sky with their radiance.

As they drew nearer to the centre of Vienna and Gisela knew it would not be long before they reached the Hotel, she said in a very small voice:

"You are . . . really going . . . away?"

"I ought to do so."

"Why . . . why? I have been so . . . happy tonight with . . . you."

"That is what makes it worse," he said, "and in a way wrong."

Gisela stiffened.

"Wrong?" she questioned.

Then in a little voice that was frightened she asked:

"Are you ... are you ... married?"

Miklós shook his head.

"No."

"Then ... why ... should it be wrong for us to know each other?"

"It is something I should tell you, but not now. I cannot bear to hurt you, and I swear, Gisela, this has been the most perfect evening of my life."

"That is ... what is has ... been for ... me."

"Oh, my darling, why can we not look forward to a thousand evenings together when we could be as happy, even happier than we are now?"

There was a note of desperation in his voice, and as she looked at him enquiringly, wanting him to explain, the horses came to a standstill and they realised they were back at the Sacher Hotel.

They stopped at the same side-entrance through which they had left, and as the footman got down from the box to open the carriage-door, Miklós said to him:

"Go round to the front and ask them to send a porter to open the side-door."

The footman hurried to obey, and Gisela said frantically:

"I must see you again! You cannot leave me like this ... wondering what could be ... wrong and not ... knowing the ... answer."

"How can we meet again?" Miklós asked.

"It is ... difficult to know when Papa will ... not be with ... me."

Miklós thought for a moment.

"If he goes to rehearsal tomorrow, you will be at the Theatre?"

48

"Yes, I shall sit . . . alone in the box."

"Then I will join you there."

"Please be very careful that he does not see you. It would be very hard for me to explain to him how we met."

"I will be careful," Miklós said. "And I know you loathe the necessity for deception as I do, when I want to tell the world that I love you."

There was no chance to say any more, for the footman had returned to open the carriage-door, and at the same moment a porter unbolted the side-door of the Hotel.

Miklós assisted Gisela to alight. Then as he walked her to the door, he said softly:

"Sleep well, my adorable nymph. Think only that you are still waltzing in my arms. Tomorrow I will see you again."

He kissed her hand, then as Gisela felt her love flow from her breast towards him, she walked into the Hotel and he turned and went back to the carriage.

In her bedroom she stared in her mirror and thought she saw the face of a stranger.

Her eyes seemed full of stars, her lips were parted, and there was a flush on her cheeks.

She knew that the beauty and the rapture of the evening were imprinted on her face.

"I love him! I love him!" she told her reflection.

Then, almost as if a cloud obscured the sun, she heard him say:

"It is wrong!"

What could be wrong? Why? What was he keeping from her?

Because he had told her to think that she was still waltzing in his arms, she pushed away the questions that beset her mind and lay down to think of him and the happiness they had found together.

* * *

Paul Ferraris was in a somewhat disagreeable mood the next morning.

Gisela was well aware that it was because he had been out late the night before and had doubtless drunk too much wine.

He was usually so very abstemious that even a glass or so more than he usually drank would give him a headache the following day, which made him irritable with her and with everybody else.

"If there is one thing I dislike, it is dress-rehearsals," he said sharply. "If they go well, things will be wrong on the opening night. If they go badly, everybody is depressed and prophesies that the Show will be a failure!"

"It could not possibly be that, Papa," Gisela said. "It seems impossible that so much talent could be seen and heard at one time on the same stage, and I know that you will receive a huge ovation."

"I doubt it," Paul Ferraris said grimly. "They are still able to hear Brahms, and I am very small-fry."

Gisela knew he was nothing of the sort. He really wanted her to reassure him, and she flattered him until he was ready to talk about his evening. To her surprise, he had not been with Johann Strauss as he had expected but with a much more important composer, Johannes Brahms.

The newspapers, especially the *Vienna Free Press*, adored Brahms, as Gisela had found as soon as she had come to Vienna.

She found they treated him as the Composer Laureate: he had received all the decorations that were obtainable, and she had the feeling that every musician in the city was trying to climb up the pedestal on which he already stood at the very top.

"Tell me about *Herr* Brahms, Papa," Gisela asked now, trying to take his mind off himself. "Will I be able to meet him?"

"Perhaps," her father replied, "but he likes to mix with the rich, the titled, and the famous. I doubt if he would be interested in a very young girl. He became my host last night only because Johann Strauss had an old friend arrive unexpectedly in Vienna."

"What did he talk about?" Gisela persisted.

"Himself and music," Paul Ferraris replied, and now there was a twinkle in his eyes.

"Tell me what he said, Papa."

"He boasted of how he is the only notable in the city to rise as early as the Emperor Franz Josef. In fact, I gather he leaves his bed at five o'clock each morning and marches through his day's programme with the self-assurance of an Emperor!"

Gisela laughed and her father went on:

"First, he tells me, he makes his own special coffee with beans sent to him by an admirer in Marseilles. Next he takes his early-morning walk, then he settles down to work."

"He is still composing?" Gisela enquired.

"Of course!" her father answered. "Most of his work is done during the summer."

"It sounds almost as if he was a man going to an ordinary office."

"That is exactly what he is," Paul Ferraris replied. "He still talks with a harsh North-German accent in a surprisingly high voice."

Again they both laughed, and Gisela realised that her father had seen the funny side of Brahm's character and was not down on his knees before the great man, as the rest of Vienna appeared to be.

They left for the Theatre at eleven o'clock, and because there was so much to do Gisela had ordered a luncheon-basket which they took with them so that her father could eat with her in the box.

She understood that most of the performers ate together, either in one of the larger dressing-rooms or else in the Green Room, to discuss what improvements they could make to their performances.

Because he still disapproved of her meeting them, she and her father would eat alone.

"Will they not think you are being very stand-offish and perhaps snobby, Papa?" she asked.

"It does not matter what they think," her father answered. "I am not having you associating with men who would not treat you in the way your mother would wish."

He sighed. Then he said:

"When we can afford it, you shall have a Chaperone who will take you sight-seeing, but for the moment I have to look after you myself."

He spoke so positively that Gisela knew there was no point in arguing with him, and anyway today she had no wish to leave the Theatre.

The break for luncheon lasted less than an hour, which was very uncharacteristic of the Viennese, who like to linger for a long time over their food and wine and even longer over their coffee.

Paul Ferraris ate very little, and on his orders there was no wine in the luncheon-basket.

Father and daughter drank water, but the Manager brought them in steaming cups of coffee from his own office.

"This is very kind of you, *Mein Herr*," Paul Ferraris said.

"I am so delighted to have you in my Theatre," the Manager replied. "Tonight all the critics will be with us and *Herr* Strauss himself has asked for a box! It will be difficult to accommodate him at the last moment."

"You have not forgotten that my daughter will require one?" Paul Ferraris asked.

"No, indeed, but I was just wondering, *Mein Herr*, if she would be so gracious as to share it with an English lady who tells me she will be desolate if she cannot hear you play."

"An English lady?" Gisela asked with interest.

The Manager nodded.

"She said she was acquainted with you, *Herr* Ferraris, many years ago, and you might remember her under the name she had then, which was Hillington."

Gisela looked at her father as he wrinkled his brow in concentration. Then he exclaimed:

"Of course—Alice Hillington—a friend of my wife's!"

"You remember her? Then would it be too great an imposition, *Herr* Ferraris, to ask you to speak to the lady, who informs me she is now called Lady Milford?"

Without waiting for Paul Ferraris to reply, he went from the box, and Gisela asked:

"Who is she, Papa? Do you really remember her?"

"She came to see your mother a long time ago when we were living in Paris," Paul Ferraris said. "You cannot have been more than five or six at the time."

The door of the box opened and a lady, very elegantly dressed and, Gisela thought, very lovely, came in followed by the Manager.

She looked at Paul Ferraris and for a moment nobody spoke.

Then with the smile which every woman found so captivating, he held out his hand.

"You are quite unchanged, Alice."

Lady Milford gave a low, musical laugh.

"I wish that were true, but it is delightful to see you again. I was so thrilled when I saw your name on the poster outside the Theatre."

Paul Ferraris kissed her hand, and as she turned to look enquiringly at Gisela he said:

"I think you will find Gisela has grown since you last saw her!"

"It must have been twelve years ago, so it is not surprising!" Lady Milford said. "You are very like your mother, my dear. Is she here with you?"

For a moment there was an awkward silence. Then Gisela said in a low voice:

"Mama . . . died two years ago."

"Oh, I am sorry!" Lady Milford exclaimed. "Forgive me for being so tactless, but I had no idea."

"We miss her, as you can imagine," Paul Ferraris said.

"How could you do anything else? She was such a lovely and lovable person. I cannot believe she ever had an enemy in the whole world."

The way Lady Milford spoke brought the tears to Gisela's eyes and she knew her father was moved too.

"I will fetch the gracious lady a cup of coffee," the Manager said, as if he thought that a cup of coffee was a panacea for aching hearts.

Lady Millford sat talking for a little while to Paul Ferraris. Then she said to Gisela:

"I should be very grateful if you would allow me to share your box with you this evening. I understand from the Manager that you sit alone."

"It would be delightful to have you with me," Gisela agreed.

At the same time, she had the terrified feeling that Lady Milford might stay with her now, and if she did it would be impossible for her to talk to Miklós and she wanted to see him more than anything else in the world.

However, to her great delight, when her father rose to go back to the stage as the Director came into the stalls and the Orchestra returned to the pit, Lady Milford said:

"I have some things to do this afternoon, but if I may join you here before the performance, it is something I shall look forward to with the greatest excitement."

"Where are you staying?" Paul Ferraris enquired.

"At the Sacher Hotel, but I only arrived this morning."

"Then that makes things very easy," he answered, "because that is where we are staying."

"What could be more fortunate?" Lady Milford enquired. "And we can all come here together."

"Yes, of course," Paul Ferraris said, "and please do not spoil the evening by staying to watch the rehearsal."

"No, of course not," Lady Milford agreed.

He opened the door of the box, and she smiled at Gisela and said:

"We will have fun together, you and I, Gisela, and it is such a pleasure to see you again and see how very attractive you have grown."

She went from the box, and as Gisela sat down she thought that Lady Milford might cheer up her father and it would prevent him from thinking of how much he missed her mother all the time.

In the past they had often entertained beautiful women, but they had not made her mother jealous.

"You do not mind, Mama, when ladies say such flattering things to Papa and sometimes seem to forget that you are there too?"

Her mother had laughed.

"I should be very jealous if I thought your father cared for them more than he cares for me," she replied. "Like all famous men, he enjoys an audience, but while he listens to compliments they pay him, I can give him something of much more importance."

"What is that, Mama?"

"The comfort and security of a home life and the love which would be exactly the same if he were no-one or even a failure."

There was a little throb in her mother's voice which told Gisela that she was speaking the truth that came from her very heart.

Then her mother went on:

"When you love somebody, Gisela, you will find that it does not matter how important they are, how successful, or how distinguished. What matters is that they themselves are a part of your heart."

Gisela thought it very commendable of her mother not to be impressed by the huge success her father had in Paris, and she knew how much she mattered to him.

After she was dead, he was like a ship without a rudder, uncertain of himself and what he should do, lonely and distraught in a manner which at times was frightening.

When they had wandered through strange countries, never staying anywhere for more than a few days, Gisela had thought her father was like a man who was searching for something he had lost and without which he was no longer the complete person he had been before.

Now she thought that in Vienna perhaps the famous musicians like Brahms with whom he could talk the same language, and someone kind and gentle like Lady Millford, would bring him peace and a reflection of his lost happiness.

The rehearsal began and once again as her father came onto the stage Gisela heard the door of the box open and felt her heart miss a beat.

Miklós sat down behind her and she knew that it would be impossible for him to be seen either from the stage or from the Auditorium.

"Have you missed me?" he asked.

It was not the question she had expected, and a faint smile curved her lips as she replied:

"I have been . . . thinking of . . . you."

"Can you imagine I could think of anything else?" he asked.

She felt as if his voice vibrated through her and her whole being was moved by the way he spoke.

"I have to see you tonight," Miklós went on. "I tried to go away this morning, but it was completely impossible for me to do so without telling you why I must go."

"How could you think of anything so horrible as to disappear without telling me why?" Gisela asked.

"Would you really mind?" Miklós asked.

"You know I . . . would."

He gave a deep sigh and she could not understand why what she had said seemed to affect him.

Then as the exquisite sound coming from Paul Ferraris's violin invaded the whole Theatre, he said insistently:

"How can we meet? I must see you."

"I expect Papa will take me home after the performance is over, and he may go to one of the many parties that have been planned, but he has not said anything, and I did not get a chance to ask him this morning."

She thought now it was rather remiss of her not to have done so, but she knew that when her father was in a bad mood he disliked having to answer questions or to plan ahead.

"I shall not be able to ask Papa exactly what he is going to do until he goes back to rest when the rehearsal is over."

"Do you think he will do that?"

"He always insists on it, and unless anything goes wrong now at this moment, he will leave when he has finished playing."

"Then he must not find me here," Miklós said. "How can you tell me what is being planned?"

"I can leave a . . . note for you with the . . . hall porter."

"Of course!" he exclaimed. "I would love, Gisela, to have a note from you! It would be something I shall always treasure when we can no longer see each other."

Gisela felt her spirits drop.

Why should he talk like that?

Why should he say things which swept away the joy that she was feeling because he was near her, the joy that was so vivid, so different from anything she had ever felt for anyone else?

She wanted to hold on to it with both hands and not let it escape her.

"Leave a note for me," Miklós said, "and I will send you one to tell you what you must do."

Gisela started.

"Please be careful. If Papa saw it he would be very ... angry, and what is more ... it would upset him before the ... performance."

"I will certainly not do that," Miklós said. "Give me your hand."

She put it at the side of her chair and he took it and kissed it.

"I love you, Gisela!" he said. "It is agony to think that I must leave you and not see you again until what will seem like a century of time. Oh, darling, do not fail me. I have to see you! I must see you!"

There was so much urgency and almost a desperation in his voice that Gisela's fingers tightened on his.

"I ... do not ... understand."

"I know that," he answered, "and I hate myself for making you suffer in any way when all I want to do is to lay the sun, the moon, and the stars at your feet."

He kissed her hand again, then before she could think of anything to say, he had left her.

As he did so, she saw her father walk from the stage and knew that he had finished playing and she had not actually heard a note of it.

They went back to the Sacher Hotel together, and as they were driving in the carriage her father talked of the congestion behind the scenes and how there were too many important performers with too few dressing-rooms.

"It is about time they had a new Theatre," he said, "but it does not sound as if it can be built for some years, and by that time half the talent with me here will be dead."

"But you would not be dead, anyway, Papa," Gisela said. "You are still a young man."

"I wish that were true," Paul Ferraris replied. "I

must remember to ask Alice Millford if she thinks I have changed since we last met."

He spoke with a faint smile on his lips and Gisela knew he was looking forward to meeting Lady Milford again.

"What are we doing after the performance this evening, Papa?" she asked.

"I have been asked to dozens of supper-parties," Paul Ferraris replied, "but I think I should take you somewhere quiet where we can eat without being bothered by a lot of people trying to talk to us."

"Oh, no, Papa!" Gisela exclaimed. "You must go to a party . . . of course you must! They will think it strange if you do not celebrate what will undoubtedly be a great success. You would not wish to get the reputation of being a recluse. That you have never been!"

"No, that is true," Paul Ferraris agreed. "In your mother's time we went to many parties and she always found them very enjoyable."

There was a pause, and it was quite obvious what he was thinking. Then he said:

"Your mother was my wife, but you are my daughter, and it makes me nervous in case you should be mixed up with the wrong sort of people, especially men."

"I am sure I shall be quite safe with you, Papa."

"One never knows," Paul Ferraris replied, "and if you would not think it very unkind of me, my dear, I would rather not introduce you to strangers until we have been in Vienna a little longer and can pick and choose whom we wish to know."

"I understand, Papa."

"Very well, Gisela," he said. "I shall take you back to the Hotel as I did last night, and if I am not too tired I will accept an invitation to one of the parties which is not likely to continue until dawn. I must not forget that I have to play again tomorrow."

"No, of course not, Papa," Gisela agreed.

Her heart was singing because she knew that now she could tell Miklós what he wanted to hear.

As soon as her father was shut in his room and she knew that he would sleep at least for a little while, she hurriedly wrote a note saying that she would be free after the Concert.

Because she felt shy, she did not start it with any endearment or sign it with her name.

Then she ran downstairs to the vestibule and gave the envelope, addressed to "*Herr* Miklós Toldi," to the hall porter.

"I do not think, *Fraulein*, there is a gentleman of that name staying at the Hotel," he said.

Gisela was just about to explain that it was the man who had come to see her at the Hotel last night, when she thought that the porter might say something in front of her father.

"He will call for it," she answered, and hurried back upstairs.

She too lay down on her bed, but it was impossible to sleep when all she could think of was Miklós and the note in his voice when he had said that he loved her, and the touch of his lips on her hand.

"I want him to kiss me again properly," Gisela told herself, and blushed because it seemed so forward.

And yet it was the truth. She knew she wanted Miklós's lips on hers and also wanted him to carry her up into the sky as he had done that first night in the darkness of the woods.

"I love him! I love him!" she told herself.

Then she realised how extraordinary it was that although she loved him with her whole heart, she knew so little about him.

He was Hungarian, his name was Miklós Toldi, and for some reason which he had not yet told her, he was trying to leave her, even though he loved her.

"Please, God, make him stay," Gisela prayed.

She knew what she would really like, even though she dared not put it into words.

Of course she wanted Miklós to ask her to marry him. She loved him and she could think of nothing nearer Heaven than to be his wife.

It might be difficult for her to leave her father, in fact it would be impossible for her to leave him altogether alone.

But perhaps in some way they could all be together, although she had no idea how it could be arranged.

But there was no point in planning anything like that or even thinking of it when Miklós had made it very clear that he could not stay with her and they had no future together.

It was as if her whole being cried out with an agony that was like a physical wound.

"I love him! I love him! How can he leave me and take my heart with him?"

Gisela felt she must cry, and as the tears gathered in her eyes, there was a knock on the door.

It took her a second or two to compose herself. Then she slipped from the bed to answer it.

She opened the door only a little way because she was wearing no more than a nightgown and a light negligee over it.

Outside there was a small page-boy almost obscured by a huge bouquet of flowers.

"For you, gracious *Fraulein*," he said in a small, piping voice.

"For me?" Gisela asked. "You are sure there is no mistake?"

"*Nein, Mein Fraulein.*"

She took the flowers from him and carried them into the room, thinking that it was very indiscreet of Miklós to send her such a magnificent basket of orchids.

They must have cost a fortune, and the basket

would be extremely difficult to explain to her father.

'Perhaps I can hide them,' she thought.

At the same time, her fingers eagerly sought for the note which, as she expected, was tied to the handle of the basket.

Then as she looked at it she saw that it was addressed just to: "Room 23," which was her room.

Her fingers shook with excitement as she opened the note, which was written in a strong, upright handwriting, and read:

> *With good wishes to a great violinist to whom I shall be listening tonight with the greatest admiration, and waiting afterwards to applaud.*

Gisela read the note, then read it again.

The message was very clear and she thought it was extremely clever of Miklós to have phrased it so that only she would understand what was implied.

He would be waiting. That was all that mattered.

She gave a little sigh of sheer happiness, then once again it was impossible to prevent the question recurring in her mind:

"Why was it wrong?"

Now in the Theatre as her father finished playing the Schubert Concerto, Gisela noted with satisfaction that he received louder and longer applause than did any of the other performers.

Lady Milford was sitting beside her, clapping enthusiastically, and as the "Bravos" rang out and Paul Ferraris returned to bow for the fifth time, she exclaimed:

"It was wonderful! There is no-one like him! You must be very, very proud."

"I am," Gisela said.

It was obvious that the audience would not let Paul Ferraris go, and as the Conductor tapped with his baton on his music-rest to alert the Orchestra, Gisela knew her father would play as an encore a melody from *The Magic Flute*, which had always been her mother's favourite.

She felt the tears come into her eyes as she remembered how much her mother had loved it.

When he finished, Gisela realised that Lady Milford was also near to tears.

"It is so moving and your father played it so beautifully," she said with a little break in her voice.

Then as Paul Ferraris left the stage and the applause began to die down, she said:

"I am determined, dearest Gisela, to cheer your father up. I can see in his eyes how much he misses your mother, but he must move back into the social life that he always enjoyed in the past."

The way she spoke made Gisela sense danger, and Lady Milford continued:

"What are you going to do after the show? I am sure your father has been asked to a dozen parties, and I would like to give one for him, and of course for you as well."

Gisela drew in her breath, and without thinking she said impulsively:

"Please, not tonight. I would love to have a party with Papa... and it is very kind of you, but... not tonight."

Lady Milford looked at her searchingly.

"You sound as if you have a reason, a very personal reason, for not wishing to alter your plans— if you have any."

Gisela did not look at her.

"That is true," she said, "but... please do not ask me any... questions. Everything has been... arranged."

"I understand," Lady Milford said, "and, Gisela, if you want my help in any way, please do not hesitate to ask for it. I loved your mother, and I expect you know that we were children together in England. Only when she married your father did we lose touch with each other, and I want to help her daughter."

"If you want to ... help me," Gisela said, "you will not say ... anything about a party ... tonight to Papa, but let him take me back to the Hotel, as he ... intends to do."

"Of course I will do anything you wish," Lady Milford agreed.

She saw how delighted Gisela was at her reply, and she added:

"But be careful of yourself, dear child. Vienna is not a city where a very young girl should be alone."

"I understand that," Gisela said, "but ... please ... tonight ... leave things just as they are."

"I have already promised you that I will do that," Lady Milford said, "and if your father asks me, which he is unlikely to do, I will tell him I am already engaged."

"Thank you ... thank you!"

She thought Lady Milford looked at her strangely, but she did not care.

All she wanted was to see Miklós, and she felt that nothing and nobody must stop them from being together for what perhaps would be the last time.

Her father had seen the flowers and been delighted with the thought that they had been sent by an unknown admirer.

"They are certainly very expensive blooms," he said. "Do you think it is a man or a woman?"

He spoke jokingly, but Gisela replied without any hesitation:

"Of course a woman, Papa!"

"I might have thought it was Alice Milford," her father said, "if in fact she had not already sent me a note wishing me luck, accompanied not by flowers but by a very fine white silk scarf which she thought I might need when the evenings grow chilly."

"How kind of her!" Gisela exclaimed.

Her father was still staring at the flowers.

"I cannot think who my unknown admirer might be," he said. "It is no-one in the Theatre, and as I have been here for only a very short time, I cannot believe that anyone from the past is aware of it."

"You have admirers all over the world, Papa," Gisela said. "Have you forgotten that you have been asked no less than three times to go to England, and you have always refused."

"The English have no appreciation of music," her father replied.

"How do you know that when you have never played to them?" Gisela enquired.

"Tonight you will hear the applause that comes from the hearts and souls of the Viennese," her father said, "and that is the sound I want to hear."

He had forgotten the flowers, Gisela thought, as they went downstairs together. Tonight meant a great deal to him, and she prayed that nothing would go wrong.

＊　　＊　　＊

Driving back from the Theatre with her father, who was almost bubbling over with excitement, she told herself that only by a hair's-breadth had she prevented things from going wrong for herself.

Supposing Lady Milford had not mentioned to her that she wanted to give a supper-party but had asked her father direct?

Gisela was sure it was indiscreet and probably a mistake to have let Lady Milford know that she had a secret, but what else could she have done?

She could only hope that Lady Milford would be loyal to her and not think it her duty to tell her father that she was doing something reprehensible.

She was sure she was safe, and yet the doubt was still there as the horses stopped outside the Hotel and her father kissed her good-night.

"I shall not be late, dear child," he said, "but Johann Strauss was very insistent that I should join him."

"I would like to meet him one day, Papa," Gisela said.

"I will think about it," her father replied. "But now that I am established, I will see that you enjoy yourself. You shall waltz, my darling, perhaps tomorrow or the next night! If you may not meet Johann Strauss, you shall at least dance to the magic of his music."

"That would be lovely, Papa!"

She kissed her father again and stepped out of the carriage.

Then as she ran in through the door she thought that nothing anybody could offer her would be so alluring, so exciting, so irresistible as the thought of Miklós waiting at the side-door.

Chapter Four

Driving beside Miklós, Gisela was almost certain where he was taking her.

At the same time, she knew it did not matter where they went as long as they could be together.

The clasp of his hand gave her a feeling of security that made her know that if she could only leave her life in his hands, she would never worry about anything again.

In her mind was the terrifying feeling that although he had said nothing yet, this was the last time she would see him and when the evening ended it would mean good-bye.

All the questions that had beset her last night, during the day, and this evening seemed contained in one word: "Why?"

But, because she did not wish to spoil the happiness of being close to him and hearing his voice, she forced herself to speak quietly and calmly, even though something inside her felt like crying out in a panic-stricken manner that she could not lose him.

"I am so delighted that your father had such a huge success," he said.

"You were there?"

"I was there, and I could see you through my opera-glasses, looking very beautiful. In fact I looked at nothing else."

"I wish I had known."

"It would have been a mistake. I knew you wanted to listen to and concentrate on your father, and, as you now know, the Viennese have taken him to their hearts."

That was true, Gisela thought. It was not only the applause that had seemed almost to rock the Theatre, nor the bouquets that were handed up to him, but the expression in the eyes of the other performers when he took his bow at the end, which told her they accepted him not only as one of them but also as one of the greatest.

She knew it would please her father more than anything else that he was accepted in the City of Music by other musicians, and she knew it would sweep away so much of his depression and unhappiness as the doors of a new world opened to him.

She wished only that she could feel the same about herself.

Instead, she felt as if doors were closing; doors of happiness which Miklós had opened briefly for her, giving her a happiness which she had a terrifying feeling would never come again in her lifetime.

Now in the light of the carriage-lamps she saw trees on either side of the road and she knew they were climbing up the hill to the Vienna Woods.

She looked at Miklós enquiringly and there was no need to ask questions.

"We met in the woods," he said, "and that is where I am taking you tonight to say good-bye."

Gisela's fingers tightened on his, and because for the moment she could find no words to tell him how much he hurt her, she could only give a little sigh that was half a sob.

As if he knew what she was feeling, Miklós lifted her hand to his lips and kissed her fingers one by one.

He did not speak and they drove on in silence until the horses came to a standstill outside what Gisela supposed was another Tavern.

It was very different from the one where they had danced last night.

Here they were so high up that the whole basin of the Danube lay beneath them. There was not a garden but a terrace with a stone balustrade over which there was an even better view than Gisela had seen from the woods near *Frau* Bubna's Inn.

The lights gleamed golden in the city, the Danube was silver, and now she realised that a new moon was creeping up the sky, adding its light to the already gleaming stars.

It was so lovely that when they sat down at the table against the balustrade, for a moment she looked at the view rather than at Miklós.

She heard him ordering food and wine. Then when they were alone and there were no other guests near them, he put out his hand towards her, saying:

"Look at me, Gisela!"

She turned her face obediently towards him, and there was the light of the stars and the moon on her hair, and the light from the Tavern windows in her eyes and on her cheeks.

"I love you!" Miklós said. "Whatever happens, whatever we have to do, I want you to remember that I love you as I never thought it possible to love any woman."

The depth of sincerity in his voice was very moving. Then, so softly he could barely hear her, Gisela whispered:

"Please . . . do not . . . leave me."

"I have to, my precious," he replied, "but before I tell you why, I want you to have something to eat and drink. You have been through one emotional experience already today."

"A very . . . happy one."

"I want you to be happy," he said fiercely. "Everything round you and near you should not only be beautiful but filled with the joy of life."

He sighed.

"That is what the Vienna Woods typify—a joy of living, which is something Hungarians understand better than the people of any other nation in the whole world."

"Tell me about your country," Gisela said.

She forced herself to say the words because in a way they were impersonal and she knew instinctively that Miklós was suffering. If he wished her to be happy, she could not bear to think that he was hurt or wounded by what he had to say to her.

"How can I explain the land I love?" he asked. "All I can say is that to me, as it is to many other people, it is enchanted."

"It is what I have always felt when I have read about it," Gisela said.

"There is something intangible and elusive about the atmosphere of the country, which is like you, my precious."

He saw the smile in Gisela's eyes, and went on:

"Perhaps it is because of your Hungarian blood."

"I am afraid there is a very little of that," Gisela said. "A great-great-grandmother is rather far away."

"But she was a Rákoczl," Miklós said, "and I suppose you know that Ferdinand Rákoczl was one of the great romantic figures of Hungarian history."

"I was not aware of that!" Gisela exclaimed. "Perhaps Papa told me about him, but I have forgotten."

"He died in 1735," Miklós said, "following a great battle against the Hapsburgs, after which he was elected leader of the country. But there was treachery, and after the death of one of his brilliant Generals he went into exile in Turkey, where he died."

"How sad!" Gisela exclaimed. "I would have liked the story to have a happy ending."

"He will never be forgotten!" Miklós said. "His dignity and humanity during his struggles and exile are always referred to by historians. I am convinced he would have made a very great King."

Gisela looked across the table with a little sigh.

"You tell the story so movingly that I feel he means a great deal to you."

"My country means a great deal to me," Miklós answered simply.

They ate and drank, but Gisela was thinking all the time of Miklós and what he had to say to her.

There was no Orchestra playing this evening, but there was soft music in the background from a piano, which seemed to mingle with the light breeze stirring the trees and to become part of the magic of the stars above and the view below.

"Every time I see you," Miklós said, "you are more beautiful than the time before, and I know it will be impossible for me ever to see another woman's face, for yours will forever be in front of my eyes."

He spoke with an infinite sadness that made Gisela feel as if a cold hand was touching her heart, and although he had not moved, it was as if he was already drifting farther and farther away from her and at any moment she might be sitting alone while he had vanished.

When she thought she must know the truth, she pushed her coffee-cup to one side and said:

"You said that you ... love me ... and I know that I love ... you, and that it will be ... impossible for me to ... love any other ... man."

She spoke in a very low voice because she was shy.

She looked at Miklós across the table and he put out both his hands to her.

"Listen, my darling one," he said, "you are not to say such things or even to think them. You have to forget me, and because you are clever and intelligent I have no doubt that that is what you will do."

Gisela shook her head.

"What I feel for you has nothing to do with my brain, except that I ... admire you and love to listen to you ... talking and ... telling me ... things."

She paused for a moment before she went on:

"My love comes from my heart and my ... soul. It is ... yours and can never be given to ... anybody else."

She saw the pain in Miklós's eyes before he said:

"I swear to you, Gisela, I did not mean this to happen."

"But it has!" she said simply. "There was nothing you or I could say or do to prevent it."

Abruptly he took his hands from hers. Then he said:

"If I touch you, it makes it harder to say what has to be said."

He turned to look with unseeing eyes at the view below them, and Gisela waited until he began:

"My name is Miklós Esterházy ..."

"You said it was Miklós Toldi!"

"I know," he answered, "but if you were a little more knowledgeable about Hungarian literature, my sweet, you would know that Miklós Toldi was the fictitious hero of a romance who was written about in 1574."

"Why did you not tell me the truth ... ?" Gisela began.

Then she stopped and exclaimed:

"Esterházy! I have heard Papa speak of them. They are a very important family!"

"Very important!" Miklós said with a faint smile. "Perhaps the most important in the whole of Hungary! At least, I like to think so."

"And you belong to that family?"

"I am the head of it, the reigning Prince."

Gisela looked at him wide-eyed and Miklós said:

"My father died last year and I, as his eldest son, and as it happens his only son, inherited the title."

He gave a deep sigh, as if it had been a somewhat arduous task, before he went on:

"We are a large family, but the succession has

gone for many years in the main line from father to son, and I have pledged myself to do my best, as my father did, for the family and for my country, for which innumerable Esterházys have fought and died."

Gisela did not speak. She only looked at him with her eyes seeming to fill her small face as he continued in a harsh voice:

"You will understand that one of the things that is demanded of the reigning Prince is that he should ensure the succession. That is why I came to Vienna."

Gisela looked puzzled and he explained:

"For years my relatives and my father begged me to take a wife, but I always thought there was plenty of time, and I enjoyed my freedom, aware that although there were many charming and delightful women in my life, I did not love them in the way I wished to love the woman who would bear my name."

Gisela had a vague idea now of what he was going to say to her, and she clasped her hands together tightly in her lap, praying that she would behave with dignity, whatever blow she had to endure.

"Because the pressure on me was so great," Miklós went on, "I came to Vienna to stay with one of my aunts who is married to a member of the Royal Family. She informed me that she had various young women in mind who would be suitable to become not only my wife but a Princess of the House of Esterházy."

Miklós drew in his breath before he said:

"The night I arrived to stay with her in her house, which is in the Vienna Woods, I went for a walk after dinner."

His voice deepened and he added:

"You know what happened. I saw a nymph standing silhouetted against the sky, and for the first time in my life I fell in love!"

"How could it . . . happen like . . . that?" Gisela asked.

Miklós made a gesture with his hands.

73

"If anyone had told me, I would not have believed it," he said. "But you know as well as I do, Gisela, that even before we touched each other there was a vibration between us, and when I kissed you I knew I had found what I had been seeking all my life."

"It was ... wonderful for me," Gisela said, "but you have ... kissed many women ... before."

"I swear before God," Miklós replied, "that the kiss I gave you and received from you was different in a way which is impossible for me to explain. It was as if we had met across time and we belonged together through all eternity."

"I ... felt that ... too," Gisela said in a whisper.

"Oh, my precious, my darling, it was so vivid to me that it might have been written on the sky in letters of fire that I had found love; a love that was different, a love that is part of God."

The way he spoke was so moving that Gisela felt the tears come into her eyes.

Then Miklós said suddenly, and his voice was harsh:

"Do not look like that—I cannot bear it! I tried to go away, I tried to leave before I should hurt you, but my love was too strong, both for me and for you."

He looked at Gisela across the table and she thought the lines on his face were suddenly deeply etched and he looked immeasurably older.

Then he said very slowly, making every word sound as if it was drawn from him in agony:

"I—love you! You are—part of me—and part of my life until I shall die—but I cannot—ask you to marry me!"

It was what she expected to hear, Gisela thought, but now that he had actually said it, it was as if he had stabbed her in her heart with a dagger.

She did not move, and yet her very stillness was as poignant as if she had cried out.

She only looked at him, and the tears that were in her eyes very slowly overflowed and ran down her cheeks.

"Oh, my God!"

Now Miklós put his hands up to his face as if he could not bear to see the suffering in hers.

With an effort Gisela wiped away the tears with her handkerchief. Then she said:

"Please ... Miklós ... darling ... do not be so unhappy. But I would like you to explain why ... when you love me ... you cannot ... marry me."

For a moment she thought he would not answer. Then he took his hands from his face and she saw that his eyes were dark with suffering.

"I will try to explain, my precious one," he said, "but it is difficult to put into words things which are bred in one's bones so that they become part of one's blood and of the very air one breathes."

"I will ... try to ... understand."

"The great families of Hungary," Miklós began, "and especially the Esterházys, are very proud. They are also exclusive in that they rarely associate with people not of the same rank. I suppose to the rest of the world we appear to live a life of exotic luxury, and our lives are certainly amusing, gay, and very extravagant."

He paused before he said:

"Our female relatives are dressed in Paris and the males have their suits made in Saville Row in London."

He gave a little laugh.

"All this sounds rather ridiculous the way I relate it to you, but I am trying to make you understand that as a family we live in a world from which we extract much that is best outside it. At the same time, we do not allow intruders through our own front doors."

He looked across at Gisela.

"You do not suppose that at night I have not

75

prayed that I could show you my possessions? I know you would appreciate the beauty of my Summer Palace in the small village of Fertöd."

Gisela drew in her breath but she did not interrupt, and Miklós went on:

"The summer-houses and the ornamental temples in the French Rococo Park would, I know, delight you, just as you would love the Opera-House and the puppet-theatre which my grandfather joined onto the Palace."

Gisela made a little murmur, and Miklós continued:

"But perhaps what you would like to see more than anything else is the Music-Room, which is so large that it is the size of an ordinary house and is a perfect background for the great musicians who have either played with or conducted the Orchestra which every Prince of Esterházy has owned."

"The Esterházys own their own Orchestra?" Gisela exclaimed.

Miklós nodded his head.

"The Esterházys have always been very cultured, and all my ancestors have employed in the Palace painters, a renowned traveller to tell tales of other lands, a Jester, and of course a *musician*."

There was something in the way he said the last word which made Gisela know that it was significant.

"The Conductors at the Palace," Miklós continued, "have included Haydn, Pleyel, and Hummel, so you can understand that as a family we have for centuries appreciated music."

He paused and Gisela said:

"I have always ... heard that Hungarians are very ... musical."

"They are," Miklós agreed. "And I expect you also know that Hungarian music itself belongs to the Gypsies."

Gisela nodded and he went on:

"For generations the Gypsies have swayed the

souls of my people with their music. They have a magic when they play their music, which is different from the music one hears in any other land."

"I have longed both to hear them play and to see them dance," Gisela said.

"I want to show you the *Csárdás*," Miklós replied. "It is a Tavern-dance originated in the Eighteenth Century, and in its music is all the Gypsy beauty, the Gypsy madness, the fierce passion and unutterable sadness."

His voice seemed to rise and deepen as he spoke, then with a tone of utter despair he said:

"And that is what I feel for you."

"Why? Why?" Gisela asked. "I . . . still do not . . . understand."

"It is agony for me to have to put it into words," Miklós replied, "but because I respect as well as worship you, it is only right that you should know the truth. Music to members of my family comes either from the Gypsies or from those who are employed and paid for their services."

Miklós's voice was clear and yet there was a note of intolerable pain in it.

"Y-you . . . mean . . . ?" Gisela faltered.

"I mean, my beautiful, adorable nymph," Miklós said, "that you would not be acceptable to my family because your father is a musician!"

Gisela drew in her breath.

For a moment she felt that she could not have heard correctly what he had said.

"I admire your father," he went on. "He is a great musician, and I know that after tonight he could take his place with Haydn, Beethoven, Liszt, and certainly with Johannes Brahms. But I could not bear you to be looked down on, snubbed, or even ostracised, as you would be if I made you my wife."

As he spoke, Gisela knew what agony it had been for him to say the words, and when they were spoken they seemed to hang in the air between them as if

77

they constituted a barrier that was impossible for either of them to pass.

Then Miklós clenched his fist and brought it down violently on the table so that the cutlery clattered.

"I have asked myself over and over again what I can do," he said desperately, "but I can find no answer."

It seemed to Gisela that she had become numb.

There were tears in her eyes, yet she thought she was no longer capable of feeling pain but knew only that she was somehow awake in a nightmare that was too horrifying to be real.

"I cannot think what I can do," Miklós said brokenly. "There appears to be no solution—no happy ending, my darling, as we both want there to be."

He threw out his hands in a gesture that was very eloquent as he went on:

"If I marry you, I know because you are sensitive and vulnerable how much you would suffer, and there would be nothing I could do to prevent it. If I leave you, I sentence myself and perhaps you to a hell that is a darkness of despair because in the time we have been together we have seen a glimpse of Heaven."

"That is . . . true," Gisela whispered. "It has been . . . like Heaven to be . . . with you."

"I tried to go away when I knew this would happen," Miklós said, "but love was too strong for me, and I could not leave you."

"And . . . now?"

"I must do what I should have done that first night after I kissed you in the woods."

He gave a deep sigh.

"I did leave, as you know, but when I was halfway home I told myself I was being a fool—you could not have been as wonderful as you seemed to be—and I came back. Then I was lost, captivated, and enthralled for all time."

"You . . . really . . . love me?"

"If I loved you less," Miklós replied, "I would marry you and damn the consequences! It is because I love you, because you are everything that is perfect, everything a man could want or desire in a woman, that I could not live and see you unhappy."

"But how can . . . I be happy . . . without you?"

"You are very young. You will forget."

"Will you do . . . so?"

"That is different."

"Not . . . really," Gisela said. "I know I am . . . ignorant about men, and I suppose very . . . unsophisticated, but the love I have for you is so overwhelming and so perfect in every way that I know that any sacrifice I have to make would be of no . . . consequence."

"That is what you think now," Miklós said, "and it is just because you are so unsophisticated, my darling, that you have no idea of the cruelty that women can inflict on each other! And men too, for that matter, in subtle ways which, small in themselves, accumulate to cause scars which can never be erased from the mind or the heart."

"I . . . understand what you are . . . saying," Gisela said, "and I suppose I must . . . admit that you are doing the . . . right thing."

"It is not the right thing for me!" Miklós protested angrily. "I love you and I want you! Your loveliness will be with me for the rest of my life."

He looked across the table and said softly:

"I will never forget that we were together and that I held you in my arms and kissed you. We could both forget the world round us, but there are my responsibilities to my people, to my family, and to those I employ. How could I serve them and at the same time protect you?"

"I can see it would be . . . impossible," Gisela said slowly. "I suppose because I am the daughter of a musician they would not allow me to fulfil the . . . duties that would be . . . expected of your wife."

79

Miklós nodded.

"That is true. There is nothing more clannish, more aggressive, or more unkind than a family who are engaged in a feud."

"You . . . sound as if this has . . . happened before."

"The Hungarians are a passionate people. When we love, we love with all our hearts," Miklós replied. "When we hate, it is an emotion which is torturous and sometimes barbaric."

He suddenly threw out his hands towards her.

"Oh, my darling, I see you are trying to understand, and I love you for it. You do not know what miseries I have been through or the agonies I have suffered already because I cannot find a way out of a dilemma which is crucifying me."

Gisela put her hands in his, and reverently he raised first one, then the other to his lips before he said:

"Come! I want to walk with you amongst the trees and pretend just for a little while that you are really the nymph I thought you to be when I first saw you, when I was a mere man, caught and enslaved by your beauty, and there was no tomorrow."

As he spoke he drew Gisela along the terrace and out into the woods where there was a path with trees on one side, and on the other sheer rocks falling for hundreds of feet down into the valley below.

They walked for some way in silence. Then there was an opening just as there had been the first time they met and behind it a little arbour made for lovers.

It brought back to Gisela so vividly the first moment she had seen him, when, trembling with fright, she had hidden from the students and he had stood in front of the opening so that it was impossible for them to notice her as they passed by.

She thought she had known in the flash of a

second that he was different and she could trust him.

And when they had talked together she had been conscious of the vibrations that seemed to link them in a manner which she could not understand, but nevertheless the vibrations were very vivid.

She was thinking now of how much he meant to her and how for the moment her brain could not realise the greatness of her love or how lost and helpless she would be when he was no longer there, when his arms went round her.

He pulled her against him very gently, then as she lifted her face to his he looked down at her in the moonlight and she knew he was imprinting her face on his memory so that he would never forget it.

"I . . . love you!" she whispered.

"And I love you!" he said. "It is an agony which tears me apart, and a glory and rapture that makes me feel we are one with the gods and are no longer human."

For a moment neither of them could move. Then, as if he could be nothing but human, Miklós's lips were on hers.

Gisela knew it was what she had been longing for since that first night when he had held her captive and she had known an ecstasy that was beyond anything she had ever imagined or thought possible.

Once again she felt a wave moving in her breasts, up to her throat, to her lips, but now it moved swiftly like a streak of lightning, half-pain and half-joy.

She knew that Miklós felt the same as his arms tightened and his lips became more demanding, more insistent.

There was a fire there too, a fire that seemed to burn its way from him until it ignited in her a tiny flame of response.

It was so beautiful and so perfect that once again it was part of the music that was playing on the breeze in the trees.

It was the song of love which only they could hear and which echoed and re-echoed within their hearts, beating frantically against each other's.

It seemed to Gisela that Miklós carried her away from the earth, its problems and difficulties, up to the sky and she was one with the moon and the stars.

The brilliance of them enveloped her until she herself shone with a light that came from the love she felt for him.

Then at last, because it was so perfect, so wonderful, beyond words, beyond even thought, she broke under the strain and with an inarticulate murmur hid her face against his neck.

She felt his lips on her hair, but he did not speak, and she knew that he felt as she did, that it was hard to come down to earth.

Instead of being one with the gods, they were a man and a woman suffering the agonies of the damned because they must say good-bye.

Then Miklós knew there was nothing more to say, nothing more they could add to a moment of rapture so poignant that it was sacred.

He took his arms from Gisela, and, taking her hand, drew her up the path which led them quickly back to the outside of the Tavern where the carriage was waiting.

Gisela stepped into it, and after the footman had shut the door, Miklós put his arms round her and held her close against him.

She knew then that they had reached the end of the symphony of their love and there was nothing either of them could do but accept it.

As he held her very tightly they drove in silence back into Vienna.

Soon there were the buildings on either side of them, then street-lamps flashing through the windows of the carriage, until they came to a standstill outside the side-door of the Hotel.

Without waiting for instructions, the footman

went round to the front entrance to find a porter to open the side-door.

It was only then that Gisela stirred and drew herself from Miklós's arms.

In the light over the door of the Hotel they could see each other's faces, and Gisela could not believe that a man could suffer as he was suffering.

The footman opened the door and they stepped out.

The porter was waiting to let them in and Gisela turned towards Miklós.

He was not looking at her. Instead his eyes were on her hands, which he held in his, and she heard him say very, very softly:

"Good-bye, my love, my only love, from now until eternity!"

Then there was the touch of his lips, and as he turned away she went into the Hotel, knowing that this was the end.

The end of love.

Only when she reached her own room did the strange numbness which had prevented her from crying or speaking as they had driven back from the woods break, and Gisela flung herself down on her bed.

She lay face down, suffering in a way that a few weeks ago she would not have thought possible.

She had been desperately unhappy when her mother died, and she had thought then that the pain of it would never leave her, but this was far worse.

While she could believe that her mother was close to her, although in another world, Miklós was still in this one, where there would be no closeness but only a separation that was not only of miles but of environment and divided interests.

She could understand exactly what he meant when he said that his family would not accept her because she was the daughter of a musician.

She had always been aware that aristocrats, even

those in France, patronised musicians and counted them as only one step higher than any other entertainer.

Johann Strauss was the Waltz King, acclaimed wherever he went, not only in Paris where everybody went wild about him, but also in London where Queen Victoria actually went to the Theatre to see him and received him afterwards.

In Boston he directed a choir of twenty thousand to celebrate the American Republic Centenary.

In Bosnia the peasants imitated his moustache, Continents waltzed to his violin, and it was as if he were leading a revolution that enthralled the Globe.

But even so, he was no more than a bourgeois in Paris, and in Vienna the Emperor Franz Josef would not meet him, nor would he reward him.

Her father was different in that he was English and a gentleman. But how did that count, Gisela wondered, when to the Hungarians he would be on a par with their Gypsies and the Conductors whom they paid to play in their great Music-Room but doubtless did not invite into the Dining-Room to eat with them.

It seemed to her that she went down in that moment into a very special hell, where she was insignificant and not good enough to walk beside those who considered their blood better than hers.

Because she had always thought of herself as the equal of anyone, now she had had not only the agony of losing Miklós but also the shock of knowing that his family would not think her good enough for him.

She could understand exactly why he would not subject her to the sneers and the patronage of his relatives, who would think her common simply because her father was a musician.

How could she and Miklós ever find happiness in a life like that?

She knew it would spoil the love they had for each other to the point where she would always be suspecting that Miklós was ashamed of her, and they would gradually lose the glory they felt now and perhaps grow to hate each other.

Every nerve of her body cried out for him, and she knew she had told the truth when she had said that no other man would ever mean to her what he meant, and she loved him not only with her heart but with her mind and her soul.

But it was not enough!

Gisela lay for a long time on her bed, and then at last, as if she had suddenly lost her youth and become very, very old, she rose slowly to undress.

She looked at herself in the mirror and it seemed extraordinary that her face had not changed. Because she was suffering so deeply, it should be deeply lined or perhaps even twisted and grotesque with pain.

Instead, her eyes were larger than ever with unshed tears, her cheeks were very pale, and it was as if a light had been extinguished within her so that in a way she was a ghost of what she had been earlier in the evening.

She knew that if she was suffering, Miklós was suffering too, and because she wanted him so intently, because she loved him with a passion that seemed to tear her in pieces, she sent her thoughts towards him as if they were carried on wings.

They were so closely attuned to each other that she was sure he would be aware that she was thinking of him and loving him.

"Oh, Miklós, I want you!" she cried in her heart.

She drew back the curtains from the window and looked out to where over the roofs of the houses she could see rising high above them the spire of the Cathedral.

It pointed the way to God, but it seemed to Gisela that God had forsaken her and brought her a glimpse of Heaven only to take it away again and leave her desolate in a darkness that would encompass her forever.

Then she prayed that she might forget and that the agony within her would pass.

Although she would always love Miklós, how could she suffer forever with the intensity that she was suffering now, which was unbearable?

She believed, with a conviction that could not be shaken, that their love was greater than time and space. She would love him and go on loving him even if he forgot her, and even if the world as they knew it came to an end.

Love was greater than anything else—love was omnipotent, powerful, indestructible.

Love was Miklós, and without him she would never be a whole person again but only a woman empty, without a heart.

It was then that she began to cry slow, agonising tears which ran down her cheeks one by one until the dam broke and they became a torrent.

Chapter Five

"Tonight," Paul Ferraris said to Gisela, "I will take you out after the Show and we will dance to the strains of a Strauss waltz."

He spoke with a lilt in his voice and made it sound as if he were giving Gisela a present of very great value.

She knew that she should respond with enthusiasm, so with an almost superhuman effort she forced herself to say:

"That will be . . . delightful, Papa! You know how much I have been looking . . . forward to it."

"You have been very good and patient, my dearest," Paul Ferraris replied. "I know how frustrating it must have been for you to be in Vienna and not to dance and listen to the tunes which Strauss has made into almost a national anthem."

He laughed and went on:

"But now you shall be rewarded. I have taken my place with the great musicians of Vienna, which is what I have worked for all my life."

"I know, Papa, and it is what Mama would have wanted."

Paul Ferraris looked round their Sitting-Room.

Since his success on the opening night, *Herr* Sacher had insisted that they move from the very small rooms they were occupying into a larger and more impressive Suite.

The Sitting-Room, furnished with mirrors, oil-paintings, and Royal Red velvet curtains, was massed with flowers from admirers.

There were small bunches of spring blossoms picked by School-children, together with huge bouquets, baskets, and vases from the music groups, Orchestras, and choirs of Vienna, and from many of its most prominent citizens.

The acknowledgement of his genius, which Paul Ferraris had missed after they left Paris, had now been returned to him a thousandfold, and despite her own personal misery Gisela was glad, knowing how much it meant to her father.

Now, when he was offering to take her out this evening to dance, she longed to refuse, feeling that to waltz without Miklós would make her cry.

However, when she had risen and dressed after a sleepless night, she had told herself that life had to go on, that her father needed her and she must devote herself to him.

She could understand now only too vividly what he had felt when her mother died.

They had been so close and their love had been so perfect that Gisela was aware it was the love that she herself wished to find with the man of her heart.

She had found it, and lost it!

Her mother had known that any sacrifice she had to make in marrying a musician was worthwhile because with Paul she possessed the most precious thing in the whole world—love.

There was no question of there ever being anybody else in the lives of either of them, and that was the sort of marriage Gisela had envisaged for herself and prayed she might find.

But now she was alone, and she knew it was a loneliness that would increase as she grew older, since nobody would ever fill the place that Miklós had occupied in her heart.

"Miklós! Miklós!" she wanted to cry, in the belief that wherever he was he would hear her and know how greatly she needed him.

Instead, she imagined him going back to his Palace, to his family, to his great Estates, the running of which would fill his days, while perhaps only at night he would think of her.

But he was a man and sooner or later the women who had amused him in the past would help him forget, and eventually Gisela would be nothing but a pale ghost whom he would perhaps remember when he heard the strains of a waltz.

Even to think of this made the tears gather in her eyes, and angrily she told herself that she should have more pride, more dignity.

Because she felt her father was disappointed by her response to his plans, she said:

"I will wear my prettiest gown, Papa, and there will be no need to come back to the Hotel. We can go straight from the Theatre to wherever you are taking me."

"That is to be a surprise," Paul Ferraris said with a smile, "but I can tell you now of something else which will surprise you. Johann Strauss has asked me if I will collaborate with him in one of his new ideas."

"Johann Strauss, Papa!" Gisela exclaimed. "It is too fantastic to believe!"

"I thought you would be surprised," Paul Ferraris said, "but he is so sure that he needs me."

"In what way?"

"The mood of his music, he believes, can now be expressed by stories enacted on stage," her father answered. "Next year he is producing an Operetta called *Die Fledermaus,* in which he wants me to appear, and before this he is following his father's practice of including Concert music in his programmes."

"It seems a very strange new career for you, Papa," Gisela said cautiously.

"I am thinking it over and I will do nothing hastily," her father said. "At the same time, Strauss will pay me double or treble what I am getting now, and money, as you are well aware, Gisela, is important."

"That is certainly something we should consider, Papa."

"That is what I am thinking," Paul Ferraris went on, "and, Gisela, now is my opportunity of making sure not only of my future but also of yours."

He saw that Gisela did not understand, and he explained:

"Although you think I do not understand money, I realised when we arrived here that we were almost down to our last schilling. That must not happen again. We must save, Gisela, at least half of what I earn every week. Then if anything happens to me you will at least not be left penniless."

Gisela gave a little cry of horror.

"Papa! How can you speak like that? You are a man with many years of work ahead of you . . . and I could not . . . lose you."

She spoke the last words with something like horror in her voice.

She had lost Miklós, and she thought now that if she lost her father as well, her life also would come to an end.

As if she needed comforting, Gisela ran across the room to put her arms round him.

"I will do anything you want, Papa, but be careful of yourself, because I love you and you are . . . all I . . . have."

Paul Ferraris kissed her forehead.

"I love you, my dearest," he said, "and that is why I have to think of your future, although because you are so beautiful I am certain you will be married sooner or later."

Gisela shook her head.

"No, Papa," she said hastily, "I have no wish to

be married. I want to be with you and to look after
you as Mama would have done if she had lived."

She saw the look of sadness that came into her
father's eyes as he said:

"If she were here now, she would have been so
proud of my success. At the same time, it would have
made no difference to what we felt for each other. In
good times or bad, we were together, and when two
people love each other, that is all that matters."

"Yes, Papa, it is . . . all that . . . matters," Gisela
murmured with a sob in her voice.

        *   *   *

Sitting alone in the box, Gisela was moved not
only by her father's playing but also by remembering
how Miklós had come to sit behind her in the shadows and plan how they could meet.

She had seen that Lady Milford was in the Theatre with some friends with whom she was having
supper later.

She was looking very attractive in a gown of
oyster-coloured satin and with diamonds in her hair.

Although she was older than the two other wom-
en who were sitting beside her in the box, she looked
so distinguished and so English that Gisela felt she
stood out, even though she made no pretence of being
as beautiful as some of the Viennese ladies.

"I must talk to her about England," Gisela told
herself. "Perhaps one day I can persuade Papa to play
in London, as he should do."

Her father's performance was greeted as usual
with tumultuous applause.

The Viennese newspapers had acclaimed him as
one of the greatest violinists there had ever been, and
many of the audience had come only to hear him.

Flowers were thrown onto the stage and Gisela
knew there would be dozens of invitations for him to
join supper-parties later.

Eventually, when the Show was over, he came to
the box and as he opened the door and she walked out

into the light, she thought that with the exception of Miklós it was impossible for her to have a more handsome and elegant escort.

In his evening-clothes, with his cape lined with red satin over his shoulders, his shining top-hat, and his gold-handled cane in his hand, she could understand why women who were passing by looked at her father and looked again with an expression of longing in their eyes.

But Paul Ferraris had eyes only for his daughter.

"I am sorry," he said, "that four encores made me late."

"I thought the audience would insist on your taking a fifth," Gisela replied.

"That is what the Stage Manager wanted," Paul Ferraris said, "but I believe always in keeping an audience wanting more, and that applies to people singly as well as in a crowd!"

As he spoke, Gisela knew he was in one of his elated moods in which he enjoyed everything, even his own jokes.

They went down the stairs and into the marble vestibule, and as they stepped into the carriage there were cheers.

Some came from members of the audience who were still waiting for their conveyances, and some from the poorer Viennese who always stood outside the Theatres at night, hoping to recognize those of importance.

Paul Ferraris waved in reply, and as the carriage set off, Gisela said with a smile:

"Johann Strauss is supposed to be the Music King of Vienna! He will be jealous of you soon, Papa."

"I doubt it," her father replied, "and I would not aspire to write the sort of music to which Strauss has persuaded the whole world to dance."

The carriage did not carry them very far, and they alighted at a doorway which was brilliantly lit

and above which was the magic name JOHANN
STRAUSS emblazoned in lights.

For the first time that day Gisela's smile was
spontaneous as her father ushered her into what she
realised was a large Dance-Hall.

It was elaborately decorated and had a balcony
all round it which was level with the Orchestra, which
occupied the whole of one end of the Hall.

In the middle was the polished floor on which
people were already dancing, and at the sides there
were supper-tables which were occupied by what
Gisela was sure were the elite of Vienna.

The women were certainly exquisitely gowned,
most wearing tiaras and some blazing with fortunes in
jewels.

It surprised her that their faces were heavily
masked by cosmetics and their eye-lashes mascaraed
to twice their normal size.

She and her father were bowed to a table where
they could watch the musicians as well as the dancers.

After her father had ordered a delicious meal and
a bottle of wine, he rose to say:

"Now, my dear, you shall dance your first waltz
in the City of Music, while it is conducted by the
Waltz King himself!"

As he spoke he looked up at the Musicians'
Gallery, and Gisela saw Johann Strauss II for the first
time.

Her first impression was that he was young and
handsome, with a head of thick dark hair parted in
the middle, heavy moustaches, and side-whiskers
which met under his chin.

Then at a second glance she realised that he was
older than he at first appeared, but she was certain he
had a charm about him that would account for his
reputation as a "lady-killer."

Her father was waiting on the dance-floor, and
Gisela felt a little guilty as he put his arm round her

and she knew this was not the first but the second time she had danced a waltz in Vienna.

She had a sudden yearning for Miklós which was so intense that she felt for the moment as if her feet would not move. Then the lilting melody of the dance seemed to take possession of her.

Strauss was playing "The Blue Danube," which had been acclaimed as his most brilliant and most successful composition.

The story of "The Blue Danube" was as romantic as that of Strauss himself.

The name had been inspired by a line from the work of a fashionable poet, but at its first performance it received only one perfunctory encore and was forgotten.

It was sixteen years later, when Strauss played in the great Exhibition Hall in Paris before Napoleon III and the Empress Eugénie, that he decided to play "The Blue Danube" waltz again.

The result was an ovation and a success that eclipsed anything he had achieved so far.

A million copies of the sheet-music were sold throughout the world with the first printing, and Gisela was told that it was "The Blue Danube" waltz that was the highlight of the performance Strauss gave in Covent Garden before Queen Victoria.

Dancing to the melody, she felt as if her feet lost contact with the ground and she was floating through the air, although she was vividly aware that it was her father's and not Miklós's arms that encircled her.

As they waltzed round the Ball-Room for the third time she felt as if the music expressed the love in her heart, and she wondered if, wherever he was, Miklós felt the same.

They went back to their table and Gisela said, because she knew it would please her father:

"Thank you, Papa. That was wonderful! I shall always remember the first time I danced 'The Blue Danube.'"

"You must say that to Johann Strauss himself," her father replied. "If you do not meet him tonight, you will certainly do so if I work with him."

Gisela paused, then said a little hesitatingly:

"It would not be in a . . . place like this . . . would it, Papa?"

"No, no, of course not," her father replied. "I would only appear in the Theatre."

As he spoke there was a loud burst of laughter on the other side of the dance-floor, and Gisela saw that a number of officers wearing colourful uniforms had just arrived.

She thought, from the way they were talking in loud voices and laughing somewhat uproariously, that they had already been celebrating.

Her father followed the direction of her eyes and exclaimed:

"Germans! They always contrive somehow to make more noise than anybody else."

This proved to be true as the evening wore on.

As Gisela and her father ate their supper, the place filled to capacity, and there were even a number of people standing near the entrance, waiting in the hope that someone who had a table would leave early.

The music was so entrancing, so gay, and so inviting that she could understand that it would be worth waiting to ensure that one could listen to anything so enlivening.

The German officers certainly needed no encouragement.

They were drinking toast after toast, and laughing so loudly that sometimes the noise they made seemed even to drown the Orchestra.

It was typical, Gisela thought, of the good-humoured Austrians that they did not seem to resent them, and in some way their exuberance magnified the laughter and chatter from the other guests.

Paul Ferraris finished his coffee, and as the Orchestra struck up another of Strauss's famous waltzes, he said to Gisela:

"Now I am feeling strong enough, as I am sure you are, to dance again."

"Of course, Papa," Gisela said with a smile. "I was hoping you would ask me."

She was just about to rise to her feet when she was aware that there was a man standing at the table.

He clicked his heels together and she saw to her surprise that it was one of the German officers from the other side of the room.

"May I have the pleasure of this dance, *Fraulein?*" he said in a guttural voice.

"Thank you, Sir," Gisela replied in her excellent German, "but I am engaged to dance with my father."

The officer laughed and it was not a particularly pleasant sound.

He was a young man, but his face was hard and he had the arrogant air that was characteristic of many of the Germans.

His looks were also not improved, Gisela thought, by the scars on his cheeks, which she knew came from the fencing-duels for which the German officers were renowned.

It was a bravado which may have given evidence of their courage, but it did not improve their appearance.

"Your—*father?*" the officer said derisively. "To dance with your father is certainly to waste your beauty and the elegant manner in which you move."

He sounded impertinent, and Paul Ferraris said sharply before Gisela could speak:

"That is enough! My daughter has already told you she will dance with me."

"But I wish her to dance with me!" the officer said. "Come!"

He put out his hand towards Gisela as he spoke, but she drew back, saying:

"No, thank you, Sir! I have no wish to dance with you!"

"But I wish you to dance with me!" the officer persisted.

There was no doubt that he had drunk enough to be aggressive, and although Gisela was sitting he now pulled her to her feet.

"How dare you touch my daughter!" Paul Ferraris thundered, rising as he spoke. "You will kindly return to your table or I will have you thrown out!"

"*You* will have me thrown out?" the officer questioned ominously.

He was still holding on to Gisela, but now he faced Paul Ferraris and there was something so frightening in his attitude that Gisela gave a little cry.

"I have told you," Paul Ferraris said, and his voice was like a whip, "to leave my daughter alone! Go back to the stable from which you have come and behave yourself!"

The officer made an audible gasp and released his hold on Gisela.

"I consider that an insult!" he shouted. "I demand satisfaction!"

"The only 'satisfaction' you will get from me is a reprimand if you do not behave yourself," Paul Ferraris replied. "I will get in touch with your Commanding Officer tomorrow and inform him of your behaviour."

"You are nothing but a fiddler," the German officer retorted. "How dare you speak to me in such a way! I have demanded satisfaction, and by God I will have it, and I will teach you a lesson you will not forget!"

His voice seemed to ring out and Gisela realised with horror that the altercation between the officer and her father had drawn the attention of quite a number of people.

They were standing round them, listening, and now the officer was joined by several of his companions who all looked as overbearing and unpleasant as he did himself.

Gisela rose and walked round the table to her father's side.

"Please, Papa, let us go," she pleaded.

"Not so fast!" the officer said. "You have not yet danced with me, and I have every intention that you will do so."

He spoke ferociously, and before Gisela could reply her father said:

"I cannot have you mixed up in this. Come, we will leave!"

"Not before you have fought me," the officer interposed. "I have asked for satisfaction and you cannot be coward enough to refuse."

He spoke jeeringly, as if he thought that was exactly what Paul Ferraris was.

Then as Gisela prayed that her father would pay no attention and would ignore the German, she heard him reply:

"If that is what you want, I am quite prepared to fight you. Where do you suggest we meet?"

The German officer laughed.

"So the fiddler has some spirit in him after all!" he mocked. "Let me tell you there is no question of us meeting anywhere. I will fight you here, and afterwards I will dance with your daughter as I intended to do ever since I first saw her."

"No, Papa ... no! You cannot do ... such a ... thing!" Gisela cried.

Even as she spoke she knew that her father was not listening, and there was an expression on his face which told her he was at his most determined.

"Very well," Paul Ferraris said quietly, "I will

fight you, and if I win, you will apologise both to my daughter and to me for your appalling behaviour, which disgraces the uniform you wear!"

"You will be the one to apologise!" the German said fiercely. "Clear a place on the floor, and I will soon have this fiddler on his knees!"

"Please, *Mein Herr*, this must not happen! Your *Exzelensies*, do not interrupt the pleasure of the evening."

It was the Proprietor pleading first with the officer, then with Paul Ferraris, but the German pushed him to one side.

Then as Gisela was speechless with horror and dismay, she saw someone placing in the centre of the floor a pair of duelling-rapiers. They were set down in a box and the German officer moved across the room to his table to divest himself of his tunic.

Paul Ferraris watched him go, and as he began to take off his evening-coat Gisela gave a broken cry.

"Please, Papa ... do not do this ... you cannot fight such a ... man. Let us go away. What does it matter if he thinks you are a coward?"

"It matters very much," Paul Ferraris replied. "I will not be insulted by a young swine who does not know how to hold his drink!"

"He may ... hurt you, Papa."

"Perhaps, but I still have to fight him."

"Papa ... please ..."

It was no use, and Gisela knew by the expression on her father's face how determined he was.

She remembered, although it was of little comfort, that he had often spoken of how much he had enjoyed fencing when he was at the University.

But that was years ago, and the German was a young man. What chance had her father against him?

"This ... must not ... happen, Papa," she said frantically. "I will dance with him!"

"Do you think I would allow a bounder like that

to touch you?" Paul Ferraris asked. "I should not have brought you here in the first place, but we are here, and we will leave with dignity."

Gisela thought despairingly that he might leave in a very different way, but there was no point in saying so.

Her father, very elegant in his thin lawn shirt and close-fitting trousers, appearing much younger than he actually was, moved slowly and without hurry onto the dance-floor.

An older, distinguished-looking man, who was obviously a person of some importance, had apparently been invited, perhaps by the Proprietor, to be Referee.

Standing at the table where he had left her, Gisela saw him speak to her father; then, joking and laughing in a boastful manner with his companions, the German officer joined them.

Without his flamboyant tunic he looked, she thought, more unpleasant than he had before, but she knew from the manner in which he looked at her father that he was sure of his victory.

Sure too that he could get his own way so that she would be forced to dance with him.

She wanted desperately to run across the floor and beg the Referee to stop the fight before it even began.

She felt she would do anything, anything rather than have her father humiliated and perhaps injured.

But she was also aware that if she behaved in anything but an exemplary manner, she would hurt his pride and must therefore remain silent.

Now everyone in the room was watching. The Orchestra had ceased to play, and it was almost as if the rest of the guests felt this was a Cabaret arranged especially for their amusement.

Gisela guessed that it was not a particularly unusual thing to happen at any of the dance-halls.

But because she was so closely involved, she felt,

as she waited for what must inevitably be a losing battle, that it was too poignant and indeed too horrible to be borne.

She wanted to hide until it was over, or at least close her eyes, but her pride forced her to hold her head high as she stood alone while the other people had moved away from her, but whether it was through consideration or condemnation Gisela did not know or care.

There was a lot of talking at the back of the Hall, and she thought perhaps people were betting on who would win the contest, and she guessed too that she was being pointed out as being the prize to be awarded to the victor.

It made her want to sink into the floor with shame.

Instead she merely lifted her chin a little higher, then fixed her eyes on her father, who was inspecting his rapier, testing it with a few strokes in the air, and his opponent was doing the same.

Then a minute later she heard the Referee say:

"In this contest, gentlemen, the first swordsman to draw blood is the winner. The fight will then cease and the dancing will recommence. You will now go to your places and be ready to start when I give the signal."

Gisela's eyes were on her father's face, hoping he would look at her, but he was instead staring at his opponent almost as if he was measuring up his character rather than his ability as a swordsman.

Frightened, desperately frightened of what might happen, Gisela began praying fervently and frantically, but somehow it was also a prayer to Miklós for help.

Then as the first sound of steel touching steel seemed to strike ominously not only in her ears but also in her heart, she found that she was not standing alone but someone was beside her.

Without even turning her head she knew who it

was; knew because her heart leapt and there were the vibrations she had known before coming from Miklós to her.

Without thinking, without even turning her eyes towards him, she slipped her hand into his and felt his fingers tighten on hers.

Her father was being cautious, while the German was aggressive.

It was almost as if he was determined immediately to frighten his opponent and overpower him before he had time to collect his senses.

But if Paul Ferraris had not fenced for many years, he still knew how to defend himself.

Every stroke the German made was intercepted, and perhaps because the amount of drink he had consumed made him not so expert in the art as he might otherwise have been, or perhaps because he wished to show off to his colleagues and such a large audience, he became wilder.

Suddenly Paul Ferraris moved from the defensive to the offensive and slipped beneath his opponent's guard.

The point of his rapier tore the German's shirt just above the shoulder and scratched his skin.

The audience, who had been silent, gave a cry and the Referee's hand went up.

"Honour is satisfied!" he exclaimed loudly so that the whole audience could hear.

Paul Ferraris lowered his rapier.

As he did so, the German lunged forward and drove into his arm.

It was a deliberate foul and there was a cry of sheer horror from those watching.

"That was disgraceful, *Mein Herr!*" the Referee said sharply to the German officer.

He turned to Paul Ferraris, who had dropped his rapier on the floor and put his left hand over his arm.

"You are the winner, *Herr* Ferraris," he went on,

"and I deeply regret that you should have been injured in a manner which I can only describe as completely unsportsmanlike."

His tone was scathing, but the German said:

"Nonsense! He tore my shirt but he did not draw blood. I am the winner and I am now prepared to claim my reward!"

As he spoke, Gisela released Miklós's hand and ran to her father's side.

"Are you hurt, Papa? Let me bandage it."

"It is nothing," Paul Ferraris replied. "A mere scratch, but we will leave now."

"Not before I have had my dance," the German insisted.

He came nearer to Gisela as he spoke, and she thought he seemed very overpowering and menacing. So much so, in fact, that instinctively she shrank nearer to her father.

Then, before Paul Ferraris could speak, Miklós was beside them and he said to the German in a tone of contempt that was unmistakable:

"If you are still determined to make a nuisance of yourself, then you will have to fight me!"

"Why should I do that?" the German officer asked. "I choose my own opponents, and I am not prepared to run through a whole Orchestra of fiddlers!"

The offensive way in which he spoke brought a sudden silence to the whole room as they waited for Miklós's answer.

"You will fight me because I tell you to do so," he replied. "If you need a reason for the contest, here is one which you will find difficult to misunderstand."

As he spoke he walked forward and slapped the German officer across the face with the white evening-gloves he carried in his hand.

The German started and exclaimed furiously:

"How dare you strike me, you scum of Vienna! I will have you know that I am Baron Otto von Hötzendorf, and I will see that you are reprimanded for such behaviour to an aristocrat!"

Again there was a silence while everyone waited to hear Miklós's reply. He answered quietly:

"Since you have introduced yourself, I am Prince Miklós Esterházy!"

Now there was an atmosphere of consternation in the whole room and Gisela heard someone behind her ejaculate:

"The champion swordsman of Hungary!"

Then, and she was hardly aware how it happened, Gisela found herself and her father seated on chairs at the side of the floor, while everyone else crowded as near as they could to the contest which was to take place.

She looked at her father and thought he seemed pale, while still holding his injured arm, but composed.

Someone had draped his evening-cape over his shoulders, and there was a glass of wine on a small table at his side should he require it.

"You are all right, Papa?" Gisela asked.

"Perfectly, and I have every intention of watching this," Paul Ferraris replied.

The Referee announced the start of the fight, and now because the German knew who Miklós was, he was concentrating and there were no sneers, jokes, or smiles as there had been before.

There was the clash of steel, then Gisela realised she was watching a master swordsman play with an inept novice in a manner which humiliated the German more effectively than any words could possibly have done.

Because he was so brilliant, Miklós tore the German's shirt again and again but without inflicting even a scratch on his skin so that the Referee would then stop the fight.

It was done almost with the rhythm of music and the elegance of a ballet, while the German floundered round, trying vainly to touch Miklós, and looking more and more foolish.

Only when Miklós finally decided he had gone on long enough did he accomplish the difficult but effective stroke that forced the rapier out of his opponent's hand so that it was thrown into the air, and the German was left weaponless.

Then the point of Miklós's own weapon touched the German over the heart, and there was nothing he could do but stand there looking abjectly humiliated.

"Now apologise!" Miklós said in a voice of command. "Both to *Herr* Ferraris and to his daughter for your appalling behaviour!"

"I—apologise," the German mumbled.

"Louder! I want everybody to hear it!" Miklós commanded.

"I apologise!"

Miklós lowered his rapier, but as he turned to thank the Referee he heard Gisela give a terrified cry.

Intent on watching Miklós and the German fight, it was only now that it was over that she looked at her father.

With an indescribable feeling of horror she saw that he was half-unconscious and a crimson flow of blood from his wound was dripping down over his hand onto the floor.

Chapter Six

Having spent a sleepless night after saying good-bye to Gisela, Miklós when he rose in the morning was determined to return immediately to Hungary.

He knew that this time there must be no question of his turning back halfway. It was his love for Gisela which told him that, agonising though it was, he was doing the right thing.

He was saving her from an unhappiness which would not only spoil their marriage but would humiliate her in a manner which he knew he could not bear to watch.

He was very fond of his relations and most of them had the happy, good-humoured nature that was characteristic of the Hungarians.

At the same time, as the Esterházys were exceedingly proud, he knew only too well how they all would fight ferociously against anyone who offended their particular code of conduct.

That Gisela was a Lady in every sense of the word would not count beside the fact that her father was a professional musician who took money for his services.

There was a great deal of musical talent among the Esterházys, and Miklós had been brought up ever since he was a small child to appreciate music and to know that it was part of his life.

However, to possess talent was a very different

thing from accepting money as a performer in front of the public, and he knew that whatever arguments he used, and whatever way he tried to persuade those older members of the family who were fond of him to be generous-minded, Gisela would still suffer.

Paul Ferraris was such a great musician, as Miklós realised on hearing him play in Vienna, that there was no doubt that the Esterházys would be prepared to accept him as a visitor in the Palace and even as a friend.

But that was a very different thing from considering his daughter as eligible to be their reigning Princess.

Ever since he had known Gisela and kissed her in the woods, Miklós had realised that she was the one woman he had sought all his life, the one person who could bring him the happiness he had always wanted.

It was not only because she was beautiful and had a character he admired and revered, but because they vibrated to each other in a manner which told him they were joined by some divine link which could never be explained in mundane terms.

It was a spiritual union and he was aware despairingly that it was something which he would never find again and which he would miss to his dying day.

He went downstairs to breakfast, determined to tell his aunt that he must leave at once.

The Grand-Duchess was having breakfast on the terrace which overlooked the garden.

It was a very beautiful garden, enshrined in the centre of the woods, and Miklós had longed to show it to Gisela.

He knew she would appreciate the romantic Rococo architecture of the house, the statues in the garden, and the peacocks which wandered through the flower-beds and trees, making everything seem even more romantic than it was already.

The Grand Duchess had in her youth been one of the most beautiful of the Esterházys.

She was still exceedingly good-looking, her white hair was exquisitely coiffeured, and she was dressed with an elegance and a *chic* that would not seem out-of-place at a garden-party in the Palace.

The Grand Duchess smiled at her nephew, which made her seem twenty years younger than she was in reality, and she held out her white hand with the grace of a ballerina.

"Good-morning my dear Miklós," she said. "I hope you slept well, and that you enjoyed your evening."

She asked the last question with a mischievous expression in her eyes because Miklós had evaded her curiosity last night when she had asked him with whom he was having supper.

He sat down at the breakfast-table, refused the dishes the servants offered him, and accepted only a cup of coffee.

The Grand Duchess noticed the lines under his eyes and his general air of depression, but she did not mention it.

Instead she said:

"I have had news this morning from your uncle. He is delighted to hear that you are visiting us, and is returning immediately from the country so that he can see you."

The information made Miklós bite back the words he had been about to utter.

He was well aware that it was a great concession for the Grand Duke, who disliked the Austrian Capital, to leave his beloved Estate and his horses, which meant more to him than anything else, especially to see him.

He told himself that if he remained in Vienna it would be agony not to see Gisela again, but for both their sakes it was something he must not do.

"It is very kind of Uncle Ludwig," he said, "but I hate to put him to so much trouble."

"The Grand Duke realises, as I do," the Grand Duchess answered, "that anything that concerns your marriage is extremely important, and we must help you in every way we can."

"I am in no hurry to get married," Miklós said quickly.

"It is something you have to do, dear boy," the Grand Duchess said, "and you are aware, as we all are, that you must have a son, and, please, God, more than one, to ensure the succession."

She saw the expression on Miklós's face and gave a little laugh before she continued:

"I know you have heard this a thousand times before, but you must be practical and do your duty to the family, and it need not be as distasteful as you anticipate."

She gave him one of her charming smiles before she continued:

"I have been thinking of where you should look for a wife, and before your uncle arrives I wish to say firmly and categorically that, whatever happens, you must not marry an Austrian!"

Miklós raised his eye-brows at this, and she explained:

"The strict protocol and stiffness of the noble families are as bad as that of the Hapsburgs themselves, and we all know how the poor Empress has suffered from them!"

The Grand Duchess's voice softened as she went on:

"I am so deeply distressed by the way in which the Empress has been treated by her horrible old mother-in-law and the Court who follow the Arch Duchess's example in making her life a misery."

"Is it really as bad as that?" Miklós asked, as he knew he was expected to say something.

"It is even worse," the Grand Duchess replied, "and the Empress told me herself that the only time she is truly happy is when she is in Hungary."

Miklós was aware of this.

He had met the Empress Elizabeth, who was spoken of as being the most beautiful woman in the world, when she was in Budapest, and he had known that only the Hungarians could give her the happiness which had evaded her ever since she had been married.

Following the confusion of the Austrian Treaty with Hungary, she had spent three-quarters of the year in the country she loved.

What was more, she dismissed all the members of her household chosen for her by her mother-in-law, the Arch Duchess, and replaced them with Hungarians.

Thinking of what his aunt had said, Miklós was sure she was right.

Although he had no wish to speak of his marriage at this moment, he did not know how he could avoid doing so, and therefore he remarked:

"Very well—no Austrians!"

"I thought you would agree," the Grand Duchess said, "and of course no French. Heaven knows how that wretched country will survive after this last invasion by the Germans."

She gave a little laugh before she added:

"And naturally I would not wish you to marry a German."

"Of course," Miklós agreed.

He was thinking of the boredom he had endured on the few visits he had made to the small German Principalities where Princes, Arch Dukes, and Margraves behaved with the pomposity of Emperors, with little or no justification for it.

There was just a faint smile on his lips as he added:

"That narrows the field considerably! So I think,

Aunt Katarina, I should go home and have a look at the Hungarians!"

"You have seen them all already, and you are well aware, as I am, that while the girls will all fight frantically to be the Princess Esterházy, it would be a mistake to choose someone so familiar, unless of course you are—in love."

Her words took Miklós by surprise, and the Grand Duchess was aware by his expression that she had unexpectedly touched a raw nerve.

Before he could say anything she added quickly:

"I am sorry, Miklós. I did not mean to pry."

As if she suddenly understood what was happening, she put out her hand to lay it on his arm as he sat beside her at the table.

"I can see that you are very unhappy," she said in a soft voice.

He did not attempt to deny it, and as she took her hand away she said, as if she would comfort him:

"Many years ago I felt as you are feeling now, and all I can tell you is that one never forgets, but there are distractions which help the time to pass."

There was so much pain as well as a note of understanding in the way she spoke that Miklós looked at her in a startled fashion.

Then vaguely at the back of his mind he remembered being told when he was quite young that his aunt had been wildly in love with one of the Foreign Ambassadors at the Emperor's Court.

He had completely forgotten it until this moment, and now he understood why this particular aunt had, despite her age, always seemed more understanding and very much more human than his other relatives.

"You say one never forgets," he remarked in a low voice.

"How could one?" his aunt questioned. "When one really loves a person, it is the nearest in this world

111

one ever gets to Heaven, and even if we have only a fleeting glimpse of its glory, we should always be grateful for having been vouchsafed anything so wonderful."

The Grand Duchess's voice was very moving, and after a moment Miklós said:

"Thank you, Aunt Katarina, for telling me that I am not mistaken in what I am feeling."

"Of course not," the Grand Duchess said, "but the world has to go on."

She paused, then she said in a very different voice:

"To get back to the nationality of your wife. I was thinking last night that Queen Victoria has made the British very powerful, and the English girls with their pink-and-white complexions and fair hair are very attractive."

As she spoke she was not looking at Miklós but was watching one of the peacocks fanning out his tail as he approached another, but she felt Miklós start as he said sharply, his voice raw:

"No—not English!"

The Grand Duchess realised that once again she had touched a raw nerve.

Gently, smoothing over the wound she had inflicted by mistake, she said:

"There are also the Danish. After all, the Princess of Wales has been an unqualified success as the wife of the Prince, who, like yourself, cannot help being a Romeo!"

Miklós tried to smile but failed. Instead he rose to his feet.

"I cannot discuss it at the moment, Aunt Katarina," he said. "Tomorrow, perhaps, but not now."

The Grand Duchess put out her hand towards him, and he took it and bent to kiss her cheek.

"You are trying to help me, I know that," he said in a low voice, "but for the moment I am suffering the agonies of the damned and am best left alone."

He walked away from her and her eyes as they followed him were very sad.

She loved Miklós more than any of her other nephews and nieces, and she had never seen him so upset before, or so unhappy.

She was sure that this was the first time he had ever been really in love, and she knew how agonising it would be when inevitably the course of true love did not run smoothly.

'I wonder who she is,' she thought curiously, and was sure she must be a very exceptional person to have captured the heart of a young man who had been pursued relentlessly by beautiful women almost from the time he was in the cradle.

"I wish I could help him," the Grand Duchess said aloud.

But she knew from her own experience that only time could do that.

* * *

Because Miklós knew he dare not go home and refuse to wait to see his uncle, and because he could not go into the city for fear that all his resolutions would be swept to one side and he could not resist seeing Gisela, he spent the next day riding and walking in the Woods.

There he was haunted by his memories of Gisela, from which it was impossible to escape. Somehow he still felt close to her and that her love gave him the courage to endure the pain which consumed him.

The Grand Duke arrived late in the afternoon of the second day and brought with him his youngest son, a young man of twenty-two whom Miklós had met several times and liked.

His name was Anton, and as soon as he was alone with Miklós he said:

"I cannot tell you how glad I am that Mama's letter, telling us of your arrival in Vienna, came when it did. It was an excellent excuse for returning to the city."

"I presume by that remark you were finding the country boring," Miklós said with a faint twinkle in his eyes.

"Dèadly!" Anton exclaimed. "Papa is making me learn how to manage the Estate, and if it amuses him to talk from breakfast to dinner of nothing but crops or the vagaries of the vines, I can think of many more amusing subjects!"

"Such as?" Miklós enquired, knowing the answer.

"Women, naturally!" Anton said. "Have you been to the Volksopen Theatre?"

"Not on this visit," Miklós replied.

"Then you must go! There is an amusing Operetta being performed there at the moment, and in it are the most alluring dancers I have seen!"

"And, of course, one in particular!" Miklós prompted.

"Of course!" Anton replied with a grin. "And tonight you shall meet her!"

Miklós would have refused, but Anton said pleadingly:

"You must come with me. If you refuse, Papa and Mama will make us stay here and we shall both die of boredom!"

"I have managed to survive so far," Miklós said.

"That is because you have been alone with Mama. She is great fun and very understanding. But with Papa she is different and she lets him drone on until sometimes I could scream!"

It was quite obvious to Miklós that his young cousin was feeling repressed, and he was not really surprised.

Uncle Ludwig, like all the Hapsburgs, was convinced that both woman and children were inferior beings and should be lectured rather than conversed with.

Because he felt it did not matter to him one way or the other, Miklós said:

"I will do anything you want, but if it is possible I shall return home tomorrow."

"Then you must certainly make a night of it!" Anton cried. "We will have dinner with Papa and Mama, then as soon as Papa starts to nod off, which he invariably does when the meal is finished, we will leave for the Theatre."

*　　*　　*

In the box at the Volksopen Theatre, Miklós tried to enjoy the dancing which was taking place on the stage and not to think that at another Theatre Gisela was sitting alone in a box.

The Shows at the Volksopen were, as he knew of old, of a very different standard from those at the Court and the other superior Theatres in the city.

The dancers, as Anton had told him, were certainly alluring little creatures, and they knew exactly how to appear enticing and inviting to the young men who took them out to supper.

With difficulty, but firmly, Miklós refused to choose another girl to make them a party of four, and he decided that as soon as they had finished supper he would slip away and leave Anton alone with his pretty partner.

He was quite certain that he could somehow ensure that the following day the Grand Duke would not be annoyed that he had returned alone.

But he knew that it was impossible for him to stay for long in the centre of the city without having an irresistible yearning to go to the Sacher Hotel to try to speak to Gisela.

When Anton had said that for supper they were going to the Café where Strauss was playing, it never entered Miklós mind for one moment that Gisela might be there.

In fact, he did not even look round the room when he entered, but concerned himself with ordering the food and wine for supper, before with a sudden

115

constriction of his heart he saw her dancing with her father.

It was such a shock that he felt for the moment as if someone had struck him on top of the head and he could not think clearly.

Then as they returned to their table he was aware that she was sitting with her back to him, and as the room was becoming more and more crowded, there was very little likelihood of her seeing him.

It was such bittersweet pleasure to look at her that Miklós wondered if he should go or stay.

Finally he decided that it would only involve him in difficult explanations if he suddenly went before he had eaten the meal he had just ordered.

Instead, as Anton and the little dancer flirted with each other with their eyes and their lips, Miklós found himself with an aching heart watching the lights bringing out the gold in Gisela's hair, and adoring the way she held her head like a flower on a slender stalk.

When the altercation began between the German officer and Paul Ferraris, he could not at first understand what was happening, until, as if Gisela drew him like a magnet, he rose and walked towards her.

Afterwards, Gisela was to think that it was fate or perhaps the power of prayer that had brought Miklós to her side at the moment when she needed him most.

It was Miklós who took charge when she realised with horror that her father had collapsed and that the wound in his arm was very much more serious than she or anyone else had realised.

It was Miklós who had Paul Ferraris carried from the dance-hall and taken back to the Sacher Hotel in the Grand Duke's carriage that was waiting outside.

It was Miklós who, with an authority which everyone obeyed, automatically procured a Doctor in record time.

And it was Miklós who instructed the valets at

the Hotel how to undress the injured man and get him into bed, causing him only the minimum amount of pain in the process.

The Doctor bound up the wound and when he had done so he came from the bedroom into the Sitting-Room to say with a serious note in his voice:

"I think, *Fraulein* Ferraris, your father will sleep now until the morning, but I shall call early and bring with me a Senior Surgeon from the Hospital whom I would like to inspect his arm."

"He is not . . . badly injured?" Gisela asked fearfully.

"Quite honestly, I do not know," the Doctor replied, "but as your father's right arm is to him so important, we must not take any chances."

It was only when the Doctor had bowed himself out, obviously impressed not only by Paul Ferraris but very much more so by Miklós, that Gisela said in a frightened voice:

"What could he mean . . . what could happen to . . . Papa's arm? Surely what he received was only a . . . flesh wound?"

"That is what we must hope, my darling," Miklós answered, "but the Doctor is quite right: we must take no chances."

"I . . . I am frightened!"

She raised her eyes to his as she spoke, and he put his arms round her.

"I will look after everything," he said. "Your father shall have the finest Surgeons that it is possible to procure, and I am sure everything will be all right."

"What will . . . happen to us . . . if he is not?" Gisela asked, and he could barely hear the words.

"There is no point in thinking about that sort of question now," Miklós said. "What I want you to do, my precious, is to go to bed and try to sleep."

She gave a little murmur as if of protest, but he went on:

"I will be back here early in the morning, before the Doctors arrive, and I promise you I will make it very clear to them that no expense is to be spared in making your father well as quickly as possible."

Gisela laid her head against his shoulder with a sigh that seemed to come from the very depths of her being. Then she asked:

"How could...you have been...there tonight just when I...wanted you so...desperately?"

"It was fate that brought me to that particular Café," Miklós answered, "the same fate that has been directing us ever since I first saw you in the woods."

"If Papa had not...fought that...horrible man, he would have...made me...dance with him."

"Forget him!" Miklós said. "The punishment I inflicted on him was one which will, because he is a German, affect his self-esteem for the rest of his life."

There was an angry note in Miklós's voice as he added:

"How dare he insult you?"

"I did not mind what he said to...me," Gisela said, "but it...hurt Papa when he...called him a 'fiddler.'"

"Of course it did," Miklós agreed.

As he spoke they were both thinking that that was the sort of disparaging way in which his family would refer to Paul Ferraris if there was any question of their being married.

Miklós's arms tightened round Gisela and he kissed her first on the forehead, then on the cheek, before he said very gently:

"Go to bed, my lovely one. Leave your father to me. I assure you nothing will be as bad in the morning as it appears now."

Gisela tried, and succeeded, in giving him a brave little smile.

"Thank you, thank you!" she said. "You are so... wonderful...and I...love you!"

"I love you too," Miklós replied in his deep voice.

He kissed her hand and left.

* * *

The following morning, as he had promised, Miklós was there almost as soon as Gisela had finished dressing.

She had not slept at all, having spent the night slipping in and out of her father's room, seeing if there was anything she could do for him.

The Doctor had obviously given him something to make him sleep, and although he had awakened and had a drink, he was still drowsy, and when she left him to dress herself, she hoped that Miklós had not forgotten his promise to come early.

She need not have worried.

He was waiting in the Sitting-Room when she came into it, but he was not alone, for Lady Milford was with him.

They were talking together, and when Gisela appeared, Lady Milford held out her hand to say:

"Dearest child, I wish you had awakened me last night. I only heard this morning from my maid what had happened, and I came at once to see if there was any way in which I could help."

"It is very kind of you," Gisela said.

"Not at all," Lady Milford replied, "because, as you know, I only want to be of assistance both to your father and to you."

She looked at Miklós as she said:

"I have learnt what happened, and it is the most disgraceful thing I have ever heard. Those swashbuckling German officers are a menace wherever one finds them."

"That is true," Miklós agreed. "And after their victory over the French, you may be quite certain they will now have ambitions to conquer the world."

"I hope I may be dead before that happens!" Lady Milford said firmly.

As if she sensed that Miklós and Gisela wished to be together, Lady Milford then returned to her own Suite.

When she had gone, Gisela found that Miklós had already ordered her breakfast to be brought to the Sitting-Room, and although she had no wish to eat anything, he insisted that she should try and at least have a cup of coffee.

However, she was with her father, who was still half-asleep, when the Doctors arrived.

There were three of them, two Surgeons and the Doctor whom Miklós had sent for originally.

There was no doubt of his qualifications, for Gisela gathered from the conversation he had with Miklós that he attended his aunt, the Grand Duchess, and was also Physician in ordinary to the Empress.

When the Doctors went into her father's room, Gisela asked if she should accompany them.

"I think it best if you wait here, *Fraulein*," the Doctor replied.

It was what she might have expected, and the moment she was alone with Miklós he took her hand in his and the warm strength of it was a comfort to her.

"It was so unlike Papa," she said in a low voice, "to lie so ... quiet ... and he ... slept as if he had not a ... worry in the whole ... world."

"I think that condition is entirely due to the Doctors," Miklós said. "I am sure it was important for him not to be restless and perhaps start the wound bleeding again."

"All this has ... occurred because Papa was trying to ... protect me," Gisela said brokenly.

"Yes, I know," Miklós said. "It was a disgraceful action, and I admired the way your father fought the drunken young fool more than I can possibly say."

"I was so worried for Papa," Gisela replied. "I knew he loved fencing when he was at the University, but that was ... years ago!"

"He has not lost his skill," Miklós said with a smile.

"When you challenged the German officer, I heard someone say that you were the champion fencer of Hungary. Is that true?"

"I won that accolade last year."

"I felt very, very proud of the way you showed the German up and made him look so foolish."

"He only challenged your father," Miklós said, "because he thought he had not even a sporting chance of defending himself. I am certain he had no idea that a musician would be able to hold his own with an officer, much less defeat him!"

He saw in Gisela's expression the horror she had felt when she knew her father was prepared to fight a much younger man.

He put his arms comfortingly round her shoulder as he said:

"It is all over now, my darling, and as soon as the Doctors give their verdict, I will go to the Theatre and tell them that your father unfortunately will not be able to appear tonight and perhaps not tomorrow. But I am sure it will only be a question of a few days."

"Yes ... I am sure ... it will," Gisela agreed. But there was a note of doubt in her voice.

They sat talking spasmodically, and yet the silences between them were not upsetting to Gisela because Miklós was there.

Had he not been there, she would have been pacing the floor and wondering what was happening in the next room.

When finally the door opened, she looked up eagerly with a smile on her lips.

The Doctor, however, merely said:

"Would Your Highness come in here for a moment?"

"Yes, of course," Miklós agreed.

He went into the bedroom, shutting the door

behind him, and Gisela thought impatiently that it was typical that because she was a woman she was excluded.

But it did not surprise her, because she was certain the Doctors were very impressed by Miklós, and he had doubtless made it clear that he was paying the bill.

'We must...pay him back...of course we must,' Gisela thought.

At the same time, she was apprehensive that the Surgeons would be very expensive, and although her father had earned a little money so far, it would not be enough.

'He must certainly get well and play with Johann Strauss,' she thought. 'He is quite right, for if he receives two or three times more than he is earning now, we can be safe, whatever our expenses may be, for a long time.'

Miklós was over a quarter-of-an-hour in her father's bedroom, and because she gradually began to grow very apprehensive, she walked up and down the Sitting-Room.

She barely noticed when the waiters came to take away the breakfast and the page-boys brought in more bouquets of flowers to add to those already filling the room.

Then at last, when she began to feel that they must have forgotten about her, the bedroom door opened and Miklós appeared.

The Doctor was not with him, and as he shut the door behind him Gisela saw his face and gave a little cry.

"What is wrong? What has happened to Papa... and where are the ... Doctors?"

Miklós stood looking at her for a moment. Then he walked to her side and very gently put his arms round her.

"You will have to be very brave, my darling."

"What has happened? Papa is not ... dead?"

122

"No, of course not," Miklós said quickly, "but I am afraid his arm is worse than we thought."

"In . . . what way?"

She knew that Miklós was feeling for words, and she cried:

"Tell me the truth! I must know the truth!"

"The truth," Miklós said slowly, "is that the point of the rapier has severed a vein, and although the Surgeons will do everything to try to prevent it, your father's arm will be very stiff and perhaps immobile for a long time."

Gisela gave a little cry of horror.

"Are you saying . . . are you telling me that he will not . . . be able to . . . play the violin . . . again?"

"It may be possible with massage and exercise, but only after months, maybe years."

Gisela shut her eyes at the sheer shock of it and Miklós held her close against him.

"I know it is hard for you to believe," he said quietly, "but it is best to know the truth."

"Poor . . . poor Papa!" she cried brokenly. "How will he feel . . . what will he do if he cannot . . . play?"

She gave a sob and it was infinitely pathetic. Then she said in a voice which Miklós could barely hear:

"And . . . what will . . . become of us?"

His arms tightened and he said:

"That is something which need not worry you. I am going to look after you, and as soon as your father is well enough we will be married."

Gisela raised her head from his shoulder and looked at him incredulously.

"M-married?" she stammered.

"I knew last night," Miklós said, "that nothing was more important and nothing mattered except our love. I will protect and look after you now and forever."

It was impossible for Gisela to answer him, but he laid his cheek against hers as he said:

"It may be hard for you in some ways, my beautiful one, but we will be together, and never again will you be insulted as you were last night in a public place, and never again will you be unprotected, because I shall always be with you."

The tenderness with which he spoke made the tears come into Gisela's eyes. Then she said:

"I shall always be proud and ... grateful that you should be so ... wonderful to me ... and ask me to marry you ... but because I admire you ... and think you the most ... magnificent man in the world ... I could never be an ... encumbrance or an ... embarrassment to you."

"You would never be that," Miklós said quickly.

"I should be," Gisela insisted, "and knowing how ... important you are, I quite ... understand that you should not ... marry anyone ... like me."

"I intend to marry you," Miklós said firmly, "and I have everything planned. I will hand over the Palace to my relatives and you and I will only go there on formal occasions when it entails entertaining a visiting Royalty, perhaps the Empress Elizabeth."

His arms tightened as he went on:

"Otherwise we will live quietly in an attractive little Hunting-Lodge that I own at the other end of the Esterházy Estates. We will not be grand, my darling, but we will be very, very happy."

"But you will be ... abdicating from your ... duty," Gisela said, "and that I ... cannot allow."

"As your husband it will be what I say and what I want," Miklós said with a smile. "And I want you, my adorable nymph, more than I have ever wanted anything in the whole of my life!"

She would have argued, but his lips closed hers and the rapture of it swept the words away.

It was only a kiss of tenderness, without passion. Then he said:

"Go to your father. I have certain things to arrange, but I will return in an hour or so."

Gisela looked at him a little uncertainly, and he lifted her hand to his lips.

"Leave everything to me, my darling. You have no problems to face. You are mine, and fate is stronger than all the arguments you or anyone else can produce."

He moved towards the outer door of the room as he spoke, and because he had told her that she should go to her father, Gisela obeyed him.

Although she told herself that it was reprehensible and wrong, there was a feeling of joy rising within her which would not be suppressed.

* * *

It was early in the afternoon, when Gisela and Miklós had finished luncheon in the Sitting-Room while Lady Milford sat beside Paul Ferraris and looked after him, that Gisela said:

"You have told me I should not ... argue with you, darling Miklós, but I want you to be very ... very ... careful before you do anything that would ... upset your relatives and ... undermine your position as head of the family."

"I have thought about it very carefully," Miklós replied, "and you are more important to me, my precious, than a million carping relatives or any possessions."

She smiled and he said:

"The musicians, the poets, the painters, the playwrights have always said that love conquers all, and who are we to disagree?"

"I love you until it is difficult for me to think clearly," Gisela said simply, "but because I love you ... I cannot bear to think that I should ... hurt you in ... any way."

She paused. Then she added:

"I ... I have something to ... suggest."

125

"What is it?" Miklós asked.

"Because I know it would be ... wrong from your ... point of view to ... marry me," Gisela replied, "perhaps Papa and I could ... live very quietly and economically in Vienna ... or in the country near the Hungarian border, until he is well enough to play again ... and perhaps you ... could often ... come and ... see us."

The way the colour rose in her cheeks and the way she stammered the words told Miklós what she was trying to say.

He knew what the suggestion meant to her, and because it was against everything she believed in, against all her purity and innocence, it told him how much she loved him.

For a moment Miklós was overwhelmed by the greatness of the sacrifice she offered; then as there was a look in his eyes which Gisela had never seen before, he replied:

"Look at me, my sweet!"

For a moment it was difficult to do what he asked, because she was shy.

Her eye-lashes flickered, the colour suffused her cheeks, then faded to leave her curiously pale, her eyes met his, and her lips trembled.

He just looked at her for a long moment. Then he said, and his voice was deep and a little unsteady:

"I worship you, my precious, because of what you have suggested to me. It tells me that your love is as great as mine and that there is nothing in the world more important than what we feel for each other!"

His voice vibrated through her as he went on:

"But I do not want only to see you occasionally in a surreptitious manner. I want to have you with me, beside me, and part of me in the face of the world. You are mine! Mine always, and I am prepared to proclaim it from the house-tops and if necessary from the peak of every mountain in Hungary!"

He spoke so vibrantly and with such sincerity that the tears came into Gisela's eyes and overflowed to run down her cheeks.

They were tears of happiness because his love was so great and so miraculous.

"I love ... you!" she said brokenly.

"As I love you!" he replied.

He put out his arms towards her as he spoke, but at that moment there was a knock on the door, and it was only after a pause that Gisela could say:

"Come in!"

"There's a gentleman to see you, gracious *Fraulein*," a page-boy announced.

"A ... gentleman?" Gisela repeated, and looked at Miklós.

It flashed through her mind that it might, although it seemed inconceivable, be someone unpleasant like the German officer.

Then she told herself it was far more likely to be someone from the Theatre, come to enquire about her father.

"What is his name?" Miklós asked.

"He says he's come from England, Your Highness," the page-boy replied. "He asked for *Herr* Ferraris, and when I said he was ill he said he'd speak to the *Fraulein*."

"From England?" Gisela echoed. "I cannot think who it can be."

"Suppose we see him and find out," Miklós suggested.

He told the page-boy to show the gentleman up, and then as Gisela rose a little agitatedly to her feet, he said:

"Do not upset yourself. Who knows? The stranger from England might bring good news!"

It suddenly struck Gisela that this was very likely.

As they had been moving about they had not

received the very small allowance which her father had been given by his father ever since he was seventeen, when he had gone to live with his grandparents in Austria.

The money had arrived irregularly, and when it did arrive, as her father often said scornfully, it was a mere pittance.

But Gisela thought now she would welcome it and thought too that because it had been delayed first during the war with France, then as they were wandering from country to country with no fixed address, it would have accumulated.

She felt her spirits rise, and when there was a knock on the door and Miklós smiled at her reassuringly, she managed to smile back.

"*Herr* Shepherd!" the page-boy announced.

He mispronounced the last word, and a small, bespectacled, middle-aged man came into the room.

Gisela thought he looked like a superior clerk, and, speaking in a precise, very English voice, he asked:

"You are Mr. Paul Ferraris's daughter?"

"Yes," Gisela replied. "But my father, I am sorry to say, is not well."

"So I understand," Mr. Shepherd answered, "but it is of the utmost importance that I should see him."

"Why?" Gisela enquired.

"My name is Shepherd, of Shepherd, Cross and Maitland, and I represent the Solicitors acting on behalf of your father's family."

Gisela was sure now that it was money that had brought Mr. Shepherd in search of her father, and because she felt it might cheer him up, she asked:

"Will you please wait a moment?"

Hurrying across the room, she opened the door of her father's bedroom.

Paul Ferraris was sitting up against the pillows, his bandaged arm in a sling, but she noticed as she entered that his uninjured hand was clasped over Lady Milford's, who was sitting beside him.

They both turned their faces enquiringly towards Gisela and she said:

"Papa, there is a gentleman here who has come all the way from England to see you. Are you strong enough to speak to him?"

"From England?" Paul Ferraris asked. "Who can he be?"

"His name is Shepherd, of Shepherd, Cross and Maitland. They are Solicitors."

"I think I have heard of them," Paul Ferraris remarked. "They must have something of importance to say to have sent him all this way."

"I think perhaps he has brought you some ... money," Gisela said in a low voice.

"In which case," Paul Ferraris said with a smile, "we will welcome him with open arms!"

"It will not be too much for you?" Alice Milford asked softly.

Paul Ferraris shook his head.

"I am too curious not to see him. Bring him in, Gisela."

Gisela went back into the Sitting-Room.

"My father will see you, Mr. Shepherd," she said, "but you must not stay long and tire him. He has been injured in the arm, and it is most important that he should rest as much as possible."

"I understand, Miss Ferraris," Mr. Shepherd replied in his precise manner, "and what I have to say will not take long."

Gisela stepped aside to allow Mr. Shepherd to enter the bedroom and she and Miklós followed him in.

The man, carrying a brief-case in one hand, walked up to the bed and bowed.

"I hear you have come all the way from England to see me," Paul Ferraris said.

"I went first to Paris, Sir," Mr. Shepherd replied,

"and while I was searching for you in vain, I was fortunate enough to read in one of the newspapers of your great success here in Vienna."

"In the newspapers!" Paul Ferraris exclaimed. "Well, I am glad that they have heard of me again."

"They were very complimentary," Mr. Shepherd said, "and the reason why I have been trying to find you, Sir, is to inform you that your grandfather is dead!"

Paul Ferraris looked at him in astonishment.

"My grandfather!" he exclaimed. "Good Heavens! I thought he must have died years ago."

"His Lordship was in excellent health until his sudden demise six months ago."

"My grandfather!" Paul Ferraris exclaimed again. "I can barely remember him!"

There was silence after he had spoken. Then Mr. Shepherd said:

"I think you must now realise, Sir, that you have inherited the title and are now the fourth Marquis of Charleton!"

His words seemed almost like a bomb-shell and for a moment they all looked at him with an expression of blank astonishment on their faces.

Finally Paul Ferraris, in a voice that seemed almost strangled in his throat, asked:

"But—my father?"

"His Lordship died a year ago. I tried to get in touch with you then, My Lord, but unfortunately there was no communication with Paris while the city was occupied."

"But my father was the younger son," Paul Ferraris managed to say.

"Your uncle was killed fighting in Egypt several years ago and it was then that your father became heir to the Marquisate. But, for reasons it is difficult to understand, he made no effort to get in touch with you."

"That is not surprising," Paul Ferraris said drily.

"He never forgave me for leaving England and living with my Austrian relatives."

"As you will understand, My Lord, we could not act without instructions."

"No, of course not."

Again there was a silence, until, as if even Mr. Shepherd found it somewhat oppressive, he said:

"My partners and I are hoping, My Lord, that you will find it possible to come to England as soon as you are well enough to travel. You will understand there are a great many matters requiring your attention."

He paused, and, as if to make certain there was no mistake, said slowly and clearly:

"Apart from the family Estate in Hampshire, Charleton House in London, and several other properties which your grandfather acquired during his lifetime, very large sums of money are involved."

Again there was a stupefied silence, and as if Mr. Shepherd understood, he added:

"If I may make a suggestion, My Lord, as I have been travelling all night to reach Vienna, I would like now to wash and have something to eat. Then perhaps, if Your Lordship is strong enough, you could look at the documents I have brought with me, which will tell you more than I can condense into a few words."

"Yes, yes, of course!"

The way her father spoke, Gisela thought, sounded as if he had a new authority in his voice.

She thought that somehow he had already assumed the air of consequence which her mother had always told her was traditionally English.

She could hardly believe what she had heard, and because it was so overwhelming she could only do what she had done before—hold on to Miklós's hand.

Mr. Shepherd, again bowing respectfully, went from the room, and as the door closed behind him Miklós said to her father:

"Let me be the first to congratulate you, My Lord Marquis. But before Mr. Shepherd entices you to England to inspect your Estates, may I beg of you to come first to Hungary for your daughter's wedding?"

For a moment Gisela thought her father was speechless. Then he laughed.

"This is certainly a day for surprises!" he exclaimed. "And so I will contribute one myself. I shall be delighted, Miklós, to give Gisela away at her wedding, as long as you will permit me to be accompanied by my wife!"

The new Marquis of Charleton looked at Lady Milford as he spoke, and raised her hand to his lips with a courteous and very foreign gesture.

Gisela gave a cry of sheer delight and, with tears running down her cheeks, ran across the room to embrace them both.

Chapter Seven

"We can leave now, my darling," Miklós said in a low voice.

Gisela, who had been watching the Gypsies and was entranced by their dancing, turned her face towards her husband and for a moment her heart seemed to stop.

Then it began beating again frantically in her breast, because the look in his eyes made her feel as if everything in the world vanished except him.

Never had she imagined that anything could be so exciting and so unbelievably beautiful as her wedding had been.

She was so entranced with everything round her that she had no idea how lovely she herself looked.

As she came up the aisle of the private Chapel of the Palace on her father's arm, Miklós, who had turned round to watch her, had felt that she really was a nymph from some mythical world who had no connection with this.

Even before they came to Fertöd, a great many things had happened which had made Gisela certain that she was living in a dream.

After Mr. Shepherd had told her father of his new position, it had taken a little time for them all to absorb the importance of it.

Even Lady Milford had realised that Paul Ferraris's status in England and in the rest of the world would be very different from what he had known before.

It was because, despite himself, he had missed his old home that Gisela was aware that now that he was the Marquis and head of the family he had lost for so many years, he would find a new happiness.

She had never understood until now how much in some ways he had resented his father's attitude towards him, and how it was that as son of a younger son he was extremely poor, whereas his grandfather as the Marquis of Charleton was very rich and his uncle as the heir could live in considerable affluence.

Lady Milford explained to her that it was traditional in England for the eldest son, because he had to keep up the dignity of the title and the huge Estates, should have everything, while the younger members of the family scraped along in sometimes quite poverty-stricken circumstances.

"It seems extremely unfair," Gisela said sharply.

"If it was not done that way, then gradually the great Estates would be sub-divided into smaller ones and the ancestral homes which are so much a feature of English life would cease to exist," Lady Milford replied.

Because her father, having run away from England and his family, had never wished to talk about them, it was only now that Gisela learnt how much Charleton had meant to him as a boy.

"I want to show you the house," he said to his daughter with an almost ecstatic note in his voice. "It was completely redecorated and a lot of it rebuilt by my great-grandfather, and then again by my grandfather."

There was a look in his eyes which told Gisela more than he could say in words.

"But," he went on, "it was a family mansion long before that, and you will find that every room is like a history-book in which the Charletons all down the ages have played a vital part."

He went on to talk of the lakes, the woods where he had played as a boy, and the stables which had contained in his grandfather's time horses which he had been allowed to ride on only very special occasions.

Now it would all be his, and the more he talked about it, the more Gisela realised that the excitement was rising in him.

"You will have to help me, my dearest," she had heard him say to Alice Milford, "otherwise I shall make a great many mistakes, not only on my own Estates but in the County."

"You have an instinct for what is right," Lady Milford had said softly, "just as you will know what is expected of you at Court, where anyway there will be dozens of people only too willing to tell you what you should do."

It was Mr. Shepherd who had said before he left for England:

"I hope Your Lordship will be able to travel soon, and I think I should add that Her Majesty has already enquired when it would be possible for you to take up your hereditary duties."

For one moment there was an expression of sheer astonishment on her father's face, then Gisela saw it replaced by one of satisfaction.

There was nothing, she thought, that her father, with his love of the theatrical, would enjoy more than playing his part at Buckingham Palace and Windsor Castle.

Also, the eager way he talked about it to Alice Milford told her that he would be very conscientious in his duties.

From her own point of view, she could only thank God every night on her knees that her father's position had so radically changed her own life with Miklós.

She had been overwhelmed by his assertion that he intended to marry her and abdicate from his important position to do so. But now it was unbelievably wonderful that she could marry him without feeling guilty.

She knew his family would now accept her as the daughter of a Marquis and that her father's musical career would be looked on as an artistic eccentricity and not as an essential profession to earn money.

It was strange to have a new name, but the more her father talked of his English family, the more she felt she had a right to it.

"You are now Lady Gisela Carrington-Charleton, dear child," her father had said, "and while the Carringtons brought a huge fortune into the family at the end of the Eighteenth Century, it was the Charletons who gained distinctions in all the great wars and who have held positions of State through the centuries."

"Now I need no longer try to prevent you from marrying me and spoiling your life," Gisela said to Miklós.

"It would have ruined my life if you had not married me," he replied. "At the same time, my darling, I am prepared to admit that it does make things very much easier."

He pulled her into his arms and said:

"It would not matter to me who you were. I realised that whatever the consequences, I could not live without you."

He then kissed her fiercely, demandingly, as if he was still afraid he might lose her and the agonies he had suffered when he tried to do so were still making him afraid.

"I love you!" he said when he raised his head. "I love you so much that I cannot think of anything except that you will be my wife and we will be together as fate intended us to be since the moment I saw you in the woods."

"A wonderful fate," Gisela said softly.

Then he was kissing her again.

There were a great many things to do before they

could be married, and it was Miklós who arranged most of them.

He even decided that if the new Marquis was to get married he should do so quietly and secretly, since the crowds, the excitement, and interviews by the Press might prove too much for him.

Because of his importance both as a musician and as a Marquis, the Mayor came to the Sitting-Room of the Sacher Hotel to perform the Civil Ceremony.

The Doctors had insisted that Paul must take the greatest care of himself and not do anything strenuous in case his wound started to bleed again.

Accordingly, while the Mayor stood, Alice and Paul sat in front of him and were made man and wife in a simple ceremony which lasted only a few minutes.

Two days later, when Paul was strong enough, they proceeded to the British Embassy Church where the English Chaplain married them in a quiet but beautiful Service at which the only witnesses were Gisela and Miklós.

After this Miklós left for Hungary to arrange his own wedding.

"If you do not join me very quickly," he said to Gisela, "I shall come back to fetch you! While you are out of my sight, I shall never feel certain that you will not vanish, and I shall have to haunt the woods night after night looking for you!"

"I will come as quickly as I can," Gisela replied, "but, darling, I have to buy some clothes so as not to shame you in front of your smart relations who buy their clothes in Paris."

She was quoting his own words to him, and he laughed before he said:

"I should adore you if you wore sack-cloth and rags, but I do know that clothes are important to a woman. I will therefore wait one week, but not a moment longer."

Gisela gave a little cry of protest and wanted to

tell him that no-one could be well dressed in a week.

But Miklós was kissing her again, and like him she thought that it would be impossible to wait any longer before they became one person instead of two.

Fortunately her Stepmother had been to Vienna before and knew who were the best dressmakers in the city.

A trousseau is always an excitement.

By promising to pay more and to give special awards to the seamstresses who were prepared to work almost twenty-four hours a day, Gisela had enough exquisitely beautiful gowns with which to leave for Hungary not quite within a week but only a few days later.

She ordered a great many more gowns to follow.

But when they finally set off, there were so many trunks to carry her purchases that her father said teasingly that she would undoubtedly be known in the future as the "Extravagant Princess Esterházy."

He was, however, delighted at her happiness and very content with his own.

There was no possibility, Gisela was sure, that anyone could ever fill her mother's place in his life after the long years they had struggled and suffered but also laughed and loved each other.

But Alice Milford had confessed that she had loved Paul ever since she had first met him, years ago, before Gisela was even born, and she was just the companion he needed at the moment.

Gisela saw Alice looking at her father with adoring eyes, and she was sure that they would enjoy together the social life that was waiting for them in England.

When they arrived in Fertöd and saw the Palace she was overwhelmed, but she was amused to see that her father with his background of Charleton took it all in his stride.

Her first sight of the huge ornamented gates which opened onto a courtyard in front of the Rococo Palace, with a staircase sweeping down on either side of the front door ornamented with urns and statues, made her feel afraid of what awaited her.

But Miklós's hand touching hers and Miklos's dark eyes looking into her blue ones told her that nothing was of any account except their love.

"Now I can show you my Palace," he said, "as I have longed to do."

"I would be very happy with you in a cottage," Gisela replied softly so that only he could hear.

"I adore you for saying that, my precious one," he answered, "and tomorrow I will make you know that whether we are in a Palace or a hut in the mountains, it is immaterial, as long as we love each other."

When Gisela saw the loveliness of the Hungarian women and especially that of Miklós's relatives, she wondered humbly how he could ever think her beautiful.

But his eyes, his lips, and the vibrations that passed between them told her it was not only a physical attraction that drew them to each other, but something divine and sacred.

Everything in the Palace was like a fairy-tale.

The next day, when Gisela was dressed in her bridal-gown by two maids who looked at her in awe and kept exclaiming over and over again how beautiful she was, she felt herself become part of the magic of Hungary.

It was a warm day, golden with sunshine, and as she looked out the window onto gardens that were brilliant with flowers, she could hardly believe that she was not dreaming or else had died and had already reached Paradise.

But that, she told herself with a little smile, she would find tonight in Miklós's arms.

There had been no need for her to buy an orange-blossom wreath in Vienna because she wore on her head a diamond tiara that was almost like a crown fashioned like a wreath of flowers which sparkled and shimmered almost blindingly in the sunlight.

The ancient lace veil she was given was so fine that it might have been woven by spiders; it flowed over her shoulders to the ground, but, Hungarian-fashion, it did not cover her face.

At the same time, she looked not only young and beautiful but pure and spiritual in a manner that made Miklós feel he should go down on his knees in front of her.

The Service in the ancient Chapel, filled to capacity with the distinguished nobility of Hungary besides the Esterházys themselves, was very moving.

The singing of the choir and the music of the organ were, Gisela knew, something which would interest her father.

Then when the wedding was over and the Gypsies played their part, she knew by the expression in his eyes that he wished he could join in on their music with his violin.

At the same time, the *Csárdás* made the bows of the Gypsies flash against the strings, causing the notes to gallop in a weird Gypsy fashion with a trembling and falling before they accelerated the pace.

The exquisite rhythm ended with a wild movement, and Gisela could understand how the dance intoxicated those who took part in it with an intensity of joy and passion.

The swirling skirts of the Gypsies, the athletic movements of the dark-eyed men, and the music that seemed to squeeze the heart were expressions of love itself.

The love Gisela knew she felt for Miklós and which she was vividly aware he had for her.

Now he had said they could go and she held out her hand to him, feeling herself quiver because he touched her.

Without disturbing any of the other guests who were all raptly watching the Gypsies dance, Miklós drew her from the gardens back into the cool shadows of the house, and a moment later the Marquis joined them.

"I understand you are leaving, my dearest," he said.

"Yes, Papa. Miklós says we can go now."

"I can understand you want to be alone. At the same time, come to England as soon as you can. I want to show you Charleton."

There was a note of pride in her father's voice that Gisela had heard before, and she put her arms round his neck and said:

"We will come, Papa, as soon as our honeymoon is over. But I want a very, very long one with Miklós."

"I can understand that," her father replied, "and Alice and I are going to honeymoon in England. It will be new and exciting for both of us, even if we have to work."

"You will love every moment of it," Gisela said as she kissed her father.

Then she kissed her Stepmother.

"Take care of Papa," she said.

"You may be quite certain of that," Alice answered, "and I promise I will try to make him happy."

Miklós said good-bye and they left the Palace by another door where a carriage was waiting.

When Gisela saw it she gave a little cry of delight, for it was open and drawn by four magnificent horses.

But the whole body of the vehicle was massed with flowers, and the awning over their head was garlanded with flowers too. The horses also had colourful wreaths round their necks and head-bands of roses.

It was so pretty that she looked at Miklós with shining eyes.

"How could you have thought of anything so fantastic?" she asked.

"I tried to think of a background for you, my lovely one," he replied.

As soon as they stepped into the carriage, as if the secret that they were leaving was carried on the air, the guests all came running from the other part of the garden to wave them good-bye.

The Gypsies played a crescendo of triumphant happiness, they were pelted with rose-petals and rice, until finally they drove away to cheers and cries of good wishes.

Some of the children ran excitedly beside the carriage until finally the horses outpaced them.

Gisela gave a little laugh.

"Our quiet departure was not very successful," she said. "Nevertheless, I loved it."

"I thought we would not upset the party," Miklós said, "but at least we avoided having to kiss all my relatives as they would have expected."

Gisela laughed, and he added:

"There is only one person I wish to kiss, and there is no prize for guessing who that is."

"Oh, Miklós, are we really married?"

"I will make you sure of that, my darling, when we reach where we are staying."

As he spoke he drew off her long white gloves and kissed her fingers one by one as he had done once before.

As he felt her tremble with a strange excitement he said softly:

"I am making you thrill, my beautiful wife, but not half as much as I intend to do later when we are alone."

They were certainly not alone for long on the journey to where they were staying for the first nights of their honeymoon.

All along the way, those who lived on the Esterházy Estate lined the route to wave and cheer, to throw flowers into their carriage, and to serenade them with music.

Several times they had to stop to receive congratulations from the Chief of a village and for Miklós to drink a glass of the special wine from the local vineyards.

Then at last they reached the house which Miklós had told Gisela he owned.

It was used as a summer-residence when the Palace seemed too hot and too formal, or when he or other members of the family wished to live simply, or just to be alone.

When Gisela first saw it she knew that it was the kind of house in which she would have preferred to live with Miklós, if it had been possible.

Of white stone, it looked almost like a Grecian Temple and it stood just above a huge lake. Sloping from the house down to the very edge of the water there were azaleas in every colour.

It was so lovely that Gisela stood entranced until Miklós suggested that, as there were now no more crowds of spectators to see them, she could take off her wreath and veil.

Gisela found that her bedroom was on the ground floor with windows opening straight onto the garden.

She thought it would be an easy way to reach the lake and swim in it, and she wondered if Miklós would allow her to do so.

Perhaps it would not be "etiquette" for the Princess Esterházy, but often when she had travelled with her father she had swum in the sea and in lakes, and she loved the feel of cool water on her body.

There were maids to help her remove her wreath and veil and tidy her hair.

The bedroom had a huge bed draped in pale blue silk, which made her think of the sky, there were white fur rugs on the ground which were very soft to the feet, while there were fat cherub-like cupids on the ceiling, and paintings on the wall.

It was a room made for love.

'This is where we will be alone together,' Gisela thought, and felt herself blush at the thought.

There was a Sitting-Room next door, or rather it was so imposing that it could be called a Salon, where Miklós was waiting for her.

Gisela ran towards him and he put his arms round her, but for the moment he did not kiss her.

"I have not had a chance today to tell you how beautiful you are," he said.

"I am . . . a little afraid . . ." Gisela whispered.

"Afraid?" he questioned.

"Because I am so happy . . . because I am here with you . . . and we are married . . . oh, Miklós . . . supposing I wake up and find you have left me . . . and I am alone . . . and I shall never see you again?"

"You are awake, my darling," he said, "and we are together, so even if we are dreaming, it does not matter."

"This is a dream-Palace," Gisela said, "and I want to look at the flowers and the lake, and, if you would let me . . . swim in it."

"I will let you do anything you like," Miklós said, "as long as you do it with me, and you love me."

"You know I love you," Gisela said. "I love you so much that it is like hearing music, and it fills my whole heart and the Universe as well."

She spoke with a note of sincerity and a touch of passion in her voice which made Miklós draw her closer and kiss her until the room seemed to whirl round her, and it was impossible to think of anything except him, his arms and his lips. . . .

* * *

Then it seemed to Gisela that only a few minutes had passed, although it might have been much longer, when the servants announced that dinner was ready and they walked into another room that lay on the other side of the Hall but still overlooked the lake.

It was painted white, with alcoves in which there were statues, and the table and everything else in the room was massed with white flowers.

It was so lovely that once again Gisela could only express her appreciation with a little cry.

They sat down at the table, but now to her surprise the servants disappeared and it was Miklós who waited on her and kissed her between every course.

There were delicious dishes, but neither of them were hungry, and after a little while they sat talking, with glasses of the famous Tokay in their hands, with which Miklós toasted her, then she him.

After that, there seemed to be so much they wanted to talk about, discuss, and plan, but somehow there were moments when words were unnecessary and the look in Miklós's eyes was more expressive than anything he could say.

Gisela knew too that he could read her thoughts and was aware how much she loved him.

There was, however, one thing she had to ask him:

"You are quite ... certain," she asked, "that your family have ... accepted Papa and ... me?"

"I wondered if you would ask me that question," Miklós said, "and I was going to explain to you, light of my life, that you need no longer be afraid that they will criticise you in any way."

He smiled before he went on:

"My family may be exclusive in Hungary, but they are very cosmopolitan, and most of my relatives have stayed in England at some time or another."

He thought Gisela looked surprised and went on:

"If for no other reason, my cousins love to hunt in

England, and the Empress Elizabeth with her enthusiasm for hunting is an Ambassador for the Shires."

Gisela gave a little laugh. Then she said:

"You were telling me what they ... feel about ... Papa."

"Yes, of course," Miklós said, "and because they have been in England so much, they know how important an English aristocrat is. As it happens, quite a number of them have met your father's father either at Buckingham Palace or with the Queen at Windsor."

Gisela gave a little sigh of relief, as if her last worry had slipped away from her shoulders.

"Apart from that," Miklós said with a twinkle in his eye, "I thought your father today looked the part!"

Gisela laughed.

"I thought that same thing, and although Papa would never admit it, he enjoys being called 'My Lord' and the even deeper bow he receives as a Marquis than he did as Paul Ferraris!"

"The world is a strange place," Miklós observed, "but while you and I can laugh at it, my precious love, we also know that it is easier to swim with the tide than to battle against it."

"But you were ... prepared to ... battle against it for ... me," Gisela said with a little catch in her voice.

"I would climb the highest mountain or dive down to the depths of the sea to have you and hold you," Miklós answered. "But today in the Chapel I thanked God from the bottom of my heart that you could be my wife without my having to be eternally on my guard to prevent you from being hurt."

"Oh, darling, darling Miklós, how can you be so wonderful?" Gisela questioned. "I told myself that I should have loved you too much to let you make sacrifices for me, but I had the feeling that I would have been weak enough to do so because I could not

146

have lived in a world of darkness and despair without you."

"I knew, when I realised you had been insulted by that swine," Miklós said, "that you were mine and I had to protect you."

He paused before he went on:

"If I loved you desperately and overwhelmingly before, from that moment in the Dance-Hall, I woke up to the fact that love has its responsibilities as well as its rapture and joy."

There was a twisted little smile on his lips as he continued:

"Very simply, Gisela, I became a man, not thinking only of myself and of you. It was something deeper, something which is so much a part of my love now that I cannot understand why I did not realise it before."

Gisela looked at him but did not speak, and he went on:

"It is the love which is the creation of life, and our lives are joined together by God, Gisela, so that we should create children born of love to carry on the world when we are no longer in it."

He spoke so seriously that Gisela was very moved. At the same time, she understood what he was saying.

"I have often thought," she said softly, "that when people marry without love and have children, they fail not only the highest and best in themselves, but their children are not so perfect as they would be... otherwise."

"That is what I know now," Miklós said, "but I only realised it when I very nearly lost you."

He put out his hand as he spoke, and as she laid hers in it and they looked at each other, she knew that they were linked so closely that not only their hearts were one but also their souls.

They had found each other through eternity, and

in the future their children, because they were born of love, would carry on the search for the perfection and love which they themselves had discovered.

Miklós lifted her hand to his lips. Then he said:

"Come, my precious."

She wondered where he was taking her, then as they moved across the Hall, she saw through an uncurtained window that the stars had come out overhead and the moon was shining on the lake.

She thought perhaps he would take her out into the garden, but instead he drew her back into the Sitting-Room and to her surprise she saw that it was unlit.

The moonlight was coming in through the windows, and now she was aware, as she had not been before, that the whole room, even as the Dining-Room had been, was filled with white flowers.

There was the fragrance of them, and they seemed almost to turn to silver in the moonlight.

Then as she stood looking round, there were suddenly the strains of violins some way away, but loud enough to fill the Salon with their melody.

As she listened she realised they were playing the tune to which she and Miklós had first met. *"I'm seeking love—"*

She felt him put his arm round her and they began to dance.

Because it was a joy to be close to him and the music was part of their love, Gisela felt as if they floated round the room and were no longer human but part of the moonlight.

As they swayed to the music, Miklós sang to her very softly, his cheek against hers:

> *"I have found love, She is not hiding,*
> *Close in my arms, She is with me*
> *High in the sky the moonlight shining*
> *Tells me how happy we'll be."*

148

Then his lips were on hers and he held her captive as they still waltzed round and round as the violins sounded like nightingales singing a song of love to the sky.

It seemed to Gisela as if they went faster and faster until finally Miklós took his lips from hers to sing:

"I have found love—sublime and enchanting,
My heart is dancing, now you are mine!"

Then he stopped dancing and, still holding her close against him, said:

"It is true, my precious. You are mine, now, tonight, and until the stars fall from the sky."

The deepness of his voice seemed to vibrate through her, and Gisela whispered:

"I love . . . you! Oh Miklós, I love . . . you!"

Now the music was playing "The Blue Danube" and as the lovely strains seemed to fill the night and ripple across the silver lake, Miklós picked Gisela up in his arms.

"The waltz of love, my darling," he said, "the waltz that we will dance together, now and forever!"

As he spoke he carried her from the Salon into the bedroom, and by the flickering light of two candles she could see Miklós's eyes with a touch of fire in them and she knew how much he wanted her.

He set her down on her feet. Then he was kissing her again, kissing her as he undid the buttons of her bridal-gown and she felt it slipping from her shoulders.

For a moment she felt shy, then she knew there was no shyness in love, only an ecstasy and a rapture to carry them both towards the stars.

As the music of the waltz grew more insistent, Gisela put her arms round Miklós's neck and he crushed her against him until it was hard to breathe.

Then as he lifted her onto the bed and a moment later was lying beside her, his lips on hers, the violins were playing very, very softly:

"My heart is dancing, now you are mine!"

ABOUT THE AUTHOR

BARBARA CARTLAND, the world's most famous romantic novelist, who is also an historian, playwright, lecturer, political speaker and television personality, has now written over 200 books.

She has also had many historical works published and has written four autobiographies as well as the biographies of her mother and that of her brother Ronald Cartland, who was the first Member of Parliament to be killed in the last war. This book has a preface by Sir Winston Churchill.

Barbara Cartland has sold 100 million books over the world, more than half of these in the U.S.A. She broke the world record in 1975 by writing twenty books, and her own record in 1976 with twenty-one. In addition, her album of love songs has just been published, sung with the Royal Philharmonic Orchestra.

In private life, Barbara Cartland, who is a Dame of the Order of St. John of Jerusalem, has fought for better conditions and salaries for Midwives and Nurses. As President of the Royal College of Midwives (Hertfordshire Branch), she has been invested with the first Badge of Office ever given in Great Britain which was subscribed to by the Midwives themselves. She has also championed the cause for old people and founded the first Romany Gypsy Camp in the world.

Barbara Cartland is deeply interested in Vitamin Therapy and is President of the British National Association for Health.

Barbara Cartland

The world's bestselling author of romantic fiction.
Her stories are always captivating tales of intrigue,
adventure and love.

☐	12273	THE TREASURE IS LOVE	$1.50
☐	12785	LIGHT OF THE MOON	$1.50
☐	13035	LOVE CLIMBS IN	$1.50
☐	13830	THE LAWN OF LOVE	$1.75
☐	14504	THE KISS OF LIFE	$1.75
☐	14503	THE LIONESS AND THE LILY	$1.75
☐	13942	LUCIFER AND THE ANGEL	$1.75
☐	14084	OLA AND THE SEA WOLF	$1.75
☐	14133	THE PRUDE AND THE PRODIGAL	$1.75
☐	13032	PRIDE AND THE POOR PRINCESS	$1.75
☐	13984	LOVE FOR SALE	$1.75
☐	14248	THE GODDESS AND THE GAIETY GIRL	$1.75
☐	14360	SIGNPOST TO LOVE	$1.75

Buy them at your local bookstore or use this handy coupon:

Bantam Books, Inc., Dept. BC2, 414 East Golf Road, Des Plaines, Ill. 60016

Please send me the books I have checked above. I am enclosing $_____
(please add $1.00 to cover postage and handling). Send check or money order
—no cash or C.O.D.'s please.

Mr / Mrs / Miss_____

Address_____

City_____ State / Zip_____

BC2—4/81

Please allow four to six weeks for delivery. This offer expires 10/81.
